He knew he was staring.

He knew it was a rude thing to do, but Hugh couldn't help himself. It almost felt as if by keeping a steady gaze on this woman, he might be able to find his balance.

It wasn't often that something knocked him sideways, but having Molly Holmes walk into his office like that had done it. He'd left the hospital yesterday quite confident that he would never see her—or her dog—again, but...here she was. In his workspace. His happy space. Not only that, she was a nurse practitioner. Someone who was highly trained enough to be filling gaps and monitoring his patients, possibly better than his more junior registrars.

Someone that he would expect to have a close working relationship with.

Hugh cleared his throat.

"About yesterday..." he began. "About your dog..."

And then he stopped because he couldn't think of what to say next.

He was still staring. At her brown eyes, which were fringed with lashes as dark as her hair. Her skin was tanned enough to make him think she spent a lot of time outdoors and...

And she was smiling at him.

Dear Reader,

My love for dogs has been lifelong, despite being bitten as a toddler because I stuck my arm through a gate to pat a Jack Russell terrier. I've had the most amazing canine companions over the years, and I'm currently lucky enough to be sharing my life with an adorable black-and-white Cavoodle called Abby, who thinks she's a small, fluffy border collie.

I have to confess that being asked to write a story featuring a therapy dog was a dream for me—especially when I discovered an elite group of dogs that are trained to go into spaces you wouldn't think they'd ever be allowed, like a procedure room, to support and comfort children.

Hugh, my hero, still thinks they shouldn't be allowed, but Molly is passionate about her work as a pediatric nurse and the handler for her beloved therapy dog, Oreo.

There's a good reason Hugh is afraid of letting either Molly or Oreo get too close to him, but once they fall in love with *him*, he really doesn't stand a chance.

Happy reading!

Alison xxx

THERAPY PUP TO
HEAL THE SURGEON

ALISON ROBERTS

Harlequin

MEDICAL ROMANCE

Harlequin®
MEDICAL
ROMANCE

Recycling programs for this product may not exist in your area.

ISBN-13: 978-1-335-94246-3

Therapy Pup to Heal the Surgeon

Harlequin Enterprises ULC
22 Adelaide St. West, 41st Floor
Toronto, Ontario M5H 4E3, Canada
www.Harlequin.com

Printed in U.S.A.

Alison Roberts has been lucky enough to live in the South of France for several years recently but is now back in her home country of New Zealand. She is also lucky enough to write for the Harlequin Medical Romance line. A primary school teacher in a former life, she later became a qualified paramedic. She loves to travel and dance, drink champagne, and spend time with her daughter and her friends. Alison Roberts is the author of over one hundred books!

For Megan

With the deepest appreciation for so many years of
your exceptional editorial skills and wisdom xxx

**Praise for
Alison Roberts**

"The love story is built up slowly but surely with just
the right amount of passion and tenderness. This
novel will tug at your heartstrings and give you hope
in miracles. All romance readers need to grab a copy
of this terrific tale ASAP."

—*Harlequin Junkie* on
A Paramedic to Change Her Life

CHAPTER ONE

IT WAS ONE of those days.

The ones where there wasn't a minute to spare and it felt like you had to focus that much harder to ensure that no time got wasted and, more importantly, that no attempt to get as close to perfection as possible got sacrificed by taking short cuts.

The kind of day that Hugh Ashcroft liked the most. When his life was exactly the way he had worked so hard to make it. The fresh appreciation for it after the interruption of taking annual leave only made a pressured routine more enjoyable. Not that he'd been lazing around on holiday. Hugh had only flown back to arrive in New Zealand yesterday afternoon, after delivering a whirlwind lecture tour in several major cities in the United States—a world away from this children's hospital in the South Island's largest city.

It was also pleasing to find he had a new, senior registrar assigned to his team. Someone who was already following his own career pathway to becoming a paediatric orthopaedic surgeon. Even better, Matthew was someone who was particularly interested in his own subspecialty of oncology.

'So I only met this seven-year-old girl yesterday.' Hugh broke the strings of the mask dangling around his neck and pushed open the doors to the operating theatre they were leaving after the successful pinning of the complicated fracture a teenager had given himself when his skateboarding trick hadn't quite worked. 'She fell over in the playground at school and came in late in the day because her leg was still painful. She had an X-ray, which ruled out any fracture, but I got an urgent call to ED.'

Hugh didn't mention that he had still been in his office at ten o'clock last night, catching up on the paperwork that had accumulated in his absence. It wasn't anyone else's business that his work filled the vast majority of his life, was it?

He pulled a clean gown on backwards to act as a coat over his scrubs and looped his stethoscope around his neck. 'I couldn't get a slot for CT and a PET scan until tomorrow morning and an MRI is booked for the afternoon but I managed to get a slot in Radiology to do an urgent bone biopsy under ultrasound and they'll be waiting for us now.'

'So you think it's an osteosarcoma?'

'Certainly looks like it. Huge lesion, just above her knee. Size of an orange. I can't believe she hasn't had problems before this.'

'The family must be terrified. What's her name?'

'Sophie Jacobs. And yes, the family is, of course, extremely concerned.' Hugh headed for the stairs rather than waiting for a lift, shoving open a heavy fire-stop door to the stairwell. 'Which is why we need to be able to give them answers as quickly as possible.'

He wasn't quite quick enough to shut down the echo of Sophie's mother's voice in the back of his head.

'But...but she's just passed her first ballet exam. She lives for her dancing...'

Yeah…'terrified' definitely summed up the parents' reaction he had witnessed last night but Hugh would never use such emotive language. He knew all too well just how devastating a diagnosis of cancer could be for a child and their family.

He knew that, if he let himself, he could be sucked back to a time when another young girl had received such a diagnosis. He would remember realising why the fight for life was called a 'battle' and the crippling toll it could take on everybody involved for months. Years, even. And, if he was careless enough, he might also get an unwelcome glimpse of that darkest of spaces when the battle was lost.

But that wasn't going to happen. Because Hugh also knew that his ability to avoid tapping into the emotions of personal memories was what made him so good at his job that getting asked to be a guest speaker all over the world was now a regular occurrence.

There were plenty of people available to provide the empathy and psychological support that was, admittedly, badly needed, but what seven-year-old Sophie Jacobs and her family needed even more were the specialists like him and his esteemed colleagues in the paediatric oncology team, who could provide the science and skill to follow through on tough decisions and provide the best quality of life for the child in a worst-case scenario and a complete cure in the best.

He was still moving fast as he reached the procedure room in the radiology department, which was another very familiar clinical space for Hugh. A glance at his watch told him he would most likely find his patient on the table with either her mother or father beside her and she might already be sedated and under the care of a team of medics and technicians. He pushed open yet another door and stepped into the room with Matthew hot on his heels.

And then he stopped, so abruptly that his new registrar very nearly collided with him.

Because he was staring at something he'd never seen in any procedure room.

Ever.

'Can somebody please tell me…' Hugh Ashcroft kept his voice quiet and he spoke slowly and very clearly so that nobody could miss the significance of what he was asking '…why there is a *dog* in here?'

Uh-oh…

Molly Holmes caught the gaze of the black and white dog sitting by her feet but if her border collie, Oreo, had picked up on the dangerous tone of this man's voice, she wasn't bothered. Why would she be, when she was so well trained to cope with anything that could happen in a clinical environment like this? Alarms going off, people moving swiftly, children screaming—none of it would distract Oreo from her mission in comforting and supporting a child. She didn't even move her chin from where it was resting on a towel on the edge of the bed, in just the perfect place for a small hand to be playing with her ear.

Molly, however, *was* bothered. Because this was the first time this was happening here and the last thing she wanted was for it to be a disaster. Thank goodness the clinical director of the entire hospital, Vivien Pryce, had chosen to observe what was going on this afternoon and she was smiling as she took a step closer to the person who'd just spoken. Molly would have thought twice about getting that close to someone who looked like a human iceberg but Vivien actually touched his arm.

'Oreo's here to help Sophie with her biopsy,' she said softly. 'Just give us another moment, would you please, Hugh? I can fill you in then.'

So…*this* was Hugh Ashcroft—the orthopaedic surgeon that everybody said was the best in the country when it came to dealing with any skeletal tumours? One of the best in the world, even? Of course it was. Molly had also heard that he insisted on doing any biopsies of his patients himself, rather than leaving it to the very capable radiology department's doctors and technicians.

Mr Ashcroft had been away on leave when Molly had started working here, having moved back to her hometown of Christchurch a few weeks ago after working in Australia for several years. Had no one informed him that the new programme of using therapy dogs in the children's hospital had been approved after apparently waiting in the wings for too long? Perhaps it had been Molly's arrival—with Oreo—that had finally tipped the balance in favour of getting the project under way?

The radiologist was on the point of inserting the cannula in Sophie's hand that would allow them to administer the sedation needed for this invasive procedure. The little girl was lying on the bed on her side. She hadn't even noticed the doctor peeling off a sticky patch on the back of her right hand, revealing skin that would now be numb from the anaesthetic cream that would make the insertion of a needle painless, because she was stroking Oreo's silky ear with her left hand.

'She's *so* pretty...' Sophie whispered.

'She thinks you're pretty too,' Molly whispered back. 'Look at the way she's smiling at you.'

'How do you know she's smiling?'

'It's her ears. See the way she pulls them down?' Talking was another distraction for Sophie from what was going on. 'You can see her teeth, too, and the way her tongue is hanging over them a bit. That's how a dog tells you they're happy and that they like you. They're smiling...'

Sophie was smiling too. So was the doctor, as she slipped the cannula into a tiny vein and taped it into position. A nurse handed her a syringe.

'You're going to start feeling a bit sleepy,' the doctor told Sophie. 'You'll be awake again very soon, okay?'

'Will Oreo still be here when I wake up?' Sophie's gaze was a desperate plea as she looked up at Molly. 'Like you said she would be?'

Molly wasn't completely sure about that now but she chose to ignore the waves of hostility she could feel coming from Hugh Ashcroft's back as he scrubbed his hands at a basin. A nurse was waiting with the gown and gloves he would need to wear to perform a sterile procedure.

'Yes,' she said, firmly. She even raised her voice a little. 'We promised, didn't we? We're not going anywhere.' She could see Sophie's eyes drifting shut as the medication was injected. 'Sweet dreams, darling.'

Oreo didn't move as Sophie's hand slid away from her ear. She would be quite happy to sit here beside the bed, as still as a rock, to guard Sophie while she had her biopsy taken, but when Molly moved back the dog followed instantly. Molly headed for the far corner of the room to tuck herself into a corner amongst the big metal blocks of X-ray machinery. Surely that would be acceptable so that she wouldn't have to break her promise to be here the moment Sophie began waking up again?

Vivien's nod suggested approval.

Hugh's glare did not. But he was glaring at Oreo, so Molly didn't get the full effect.

'We can discuss this later.' Hugh's tone was dismissive but his tone as he turned to Sophie's mother was noticeably warmer. 'Hi, Joanne. I'm sorry I couldn't get here any sooner.'

'It's okay.' Joanne stroked her daughter's wispy blonde curls. 'I can't believe how easy it's been with having Oreo able to be with her. Sophie just adores dogs… Dancing and dogs are her two favourite things in the world.'

'Mmm.'

The sound from Hugh was strangled enough for Molly to start feeling nervous about the upcoming discussion that she would, no doubt, be part of. She caught Vivien's glance as Hugh, now gowned and gloved, stepped towards the table and the older woman's expression was reassuring. Moments later, however, the beeping of a pager saw the clinical director reaching for the message and then mouthing an apology to Molly as she slipped out of the room.

Sorry…have to go…

Molly would have loved to have followed her but she'd made a promise to Sophie and wasn't about to break it. She knew she had Vivien's support. It had been Vivien who'd signed off on Molly using her highly trained dog for an extension of duties that went quite a long way above any simple animal therapy programme that allowed dogs to visit public areas of a hospital or even within the wards. Using medical assistance dogs, or 'dogtors' as they were affectionally known, was happening more and more overseas but Oreo was one of the first dogs in this country to be approved to enter clinical areas like this procedure room, recovery areas and even the intensive care unit to assist children. Molly had made the dog version of a gown Oreo was wearing to cover her back and the elastic topped booties for her paws, which were a smaller size of the disposable ones available for staff to put over their footwear.

Sophie was lying on her back now with an area of her upper leg being prepped. An ultrasound technician was manoeuvring her equipment into place and a nurse was uncovering the top of a sterile trolley that had all the instruments and other supplies that would be needed, including the jars to hold the fragments of bone tissue about to be collected.

'You don't have to watch this bit, Joanne, if you'd rather not.' Hugh looked away from the screen as the technician located the bone lesion. They were ready to begin the procedure. The biopsy needle would show up on the screen to let him position it so that they could be confident the samples would be coming from exactly the right spot.

'I won't watch,' Joanne said quietly. 'But I'd like to stay close. Just in case Sophie might know if I'm not here.' She turned to face the head of the bed so she couldn't see what was happening and she bent down so that she was curled protectively over her daughter, her lips touching Sophie's hair. 'Mummy's here, sweetheart. It's okay... I'm here...'

Molly blinked back a tear but she could feel herself nodding at the idea that Sophie might be aware of her mother's touch. During the later stages of Oreo's training in Australia, she'd seen children respond to the dog's presence even when they were deeply unconscious and on a ventilator in ICU. She'd seen their heart rate and blood pressure drop after just a few minutes of their fingers being in contact with the soft warmth of Oreo's body.

She couldn't see the screen of the machine monitoring Sophie's heart rate and blood pressure so Molly watched Hugh instead. He certainly seemed to know what he was doing and she knew he was so focussed he'd totally forgotten her—and Oreo's—presence in the room. He was calm and confident, making a small incision on Sophie's leg and inserting the device that placed a cannula down to bone level.

'Drill, thanks.' Hugh smoothly removed the stylet and went on to the next stage of the procedure to make an opening in the bone, his gaze on the screen to get right inside the tumour. 'This won't take much longer,' he told Joanne. 'I'm about to start collecting the samples. I'll have an eleven-gauge biopsy needle, please,' he said to his scrub nurse.

Molly could see the care he took to remove several samples of tissue and ease them into the collection jars. She knew some would be used for tissue-based diagnosis and others for molecular analysis. If this tumour was malignant, they would soon know just how dangerous it might be. Again, her heart squeezed painfully enough to bring tears to her eyes. Molly might not be a mother herself, yet, but she was an aunty to nieces and nephews whom she adored and she had chosen to become a paediatric nurse because of her love for children. The joy of sharing their journey back to health was the best feeling ever but being part of the challenge of caring for them when they faced—and sometimes lost—a battle for life was as much of a privilege as it was heartbreaking.

She could feel a tear tickling as it ran down the side of her nose. Without thinking, she reached up to wipe it away with her fingers. She knew she hadn't made a sound, like a sniff or something, so it had to be purely coincidence that Hugh Ashcroft looked in her direction at that particular moment as he stepped back from finishing the procedure.

Molly could only see his eyes between the top

of the mask and the cap that was covering his hair, but that was enough to know that he was even less impressed than he had been when he'd seen Oreo in here.

The sedation for Sophie was already wearing off as a nurse put a dressing over the wound on her leg. The little girl was turning her head.

'Where's Oreo…?'

'Right here, darling…' Molly moved back towards the bed with Oreo glued to her leg. 'We're going to go back to the ward with you.'

Oreo put her chin on the edge of the mattress again. Her plume of a tail waved gently as she felt the touch of Sophie's hand on her head.

'Can she sleep with me tonight?'

A sound that was reminiscent of a growl came from Hugh's direction but maybe he was having trouble stripping off his gloves and gown. Or perhaps he was simply clearing his throat before speaking quietly to Sophie's mother about how long it would take for the pathology results to come through.

Molly had to shake her head. 'Sorry,' she said to Sophie. 'We can come back to the ward with you for a bit but there are special rules for dogs that visit in the hospital and Oreo's got to come home with me to sleep.'

Behind her, she could hear Joanne being told that an MRI and PET scan were booked for tomorrow and her heart sank. The surgeon had to be already very confident of his diagnosis if he wanted the kind of diagnostic tests that would let them stage the cancer by checking for its spread to other parts of the body like the liver or lungs.

Molly made her tone bright. 'Hey…did I hear your mum say that you love dancing, Sophie?'

Sophie's nod was drowsy.

'So does Oreo.'

Sophie dragged her eyes open again. 'Dogs can't dance…'

'Oreo can. We'll show you when she comes to visit one day.'

'Promise…?'

Molly didn't shift her gaze but she could hear that the conversation with Sophie's mum had ended and she could feel the stare coming in her direction from the orthopaedic surgeon, who was now listening to what she was saying.

It was already clear that Hugh Ashcroft didn't like dogs. Or women crying. But it wouldn't be the first time that she'd encountered a surgeon who found it difficult to show a bit of compassion. Maybe it was because their patients were unconscious for most of the time they spent with them so it was easier to be aloof? To see them as simply patients needing surgical treatment without the complications of their own lives and families or their dreams and fears that could make a situation unbearable. And maybe it was just as well there were people like her around to balance the equation.

'I promise,' she whispered to Sophie.

She looked up as she heard another pager beeping, just in time to see Hugh Ashcroft leaving the procedure room.

He spotted her heading through the hospital foyer towards the main doors.

It wasn't hard. Not when she had that large black and white dog walking beside her. At least the animal wasn't still dressed up in a ridiculous version of a human's theatre gown and booties now. It was wearing a red coat with white writing that advertised its status as a service dog. It also had the medical logo of a heart divided by a stylised ECG trace. And…good grief…small dog paw prints beneath it?

'Excuse me…' It was a command rather than a query.

She turned. She'd been wearing a hat and mask in the procedure room so he hadn't really seen what she looked like and Hugh's first impression was of very curly dark hair that was almost shoulder length and quite uncontrolled looking. Wild, even…

He got closer. 'I'm Hugh Ashcroft,' he introduced himself.

'Yes, I know.'

She had hazel-brown eyes and he could see the flash of wariness in them, which was understandable, given that he'd heard her making a promise to a sick child that—when Vivien had heard his misgivings about the access her dog had been granted in visiting *his* patients—she might no longer be able to keep.

'I'm just on my way to find Vivien Pryce. I saw you and realised I don't actually know your name.'

'Molly,' she said. 'Molly Holmes. But I think you'll find that Dr Pryce is not available. I was supposed to meet her myself so that we could talk about our first session with a dogtor.'

'With a…*what*?'

'Medical assistance dogs. Calling them "dogtors" differentiates them from the pet therapy dogs that don't have the level of training needed to go into a clinical environment.'

The dog at her feet was looking up at Hugh and he got the strange notion that he was being approved of. Being smiled at, even? Perhaps that was because the dog was wagging its tail as it stared at him—a slow, thoughtful sweep against the polished linoleum. Its ears were pulled back as well, which made its eyes crinkle, just as a person's might if they were really happy to see someone they knew. Hugh didn't smile back. He avoided direct eye contact and stared at the dog's owner instead.

'Dogtors' was just the kind of cute title he might have expected people involved with this sort of organisation to have come up with. People who probably also spent a significant percentage of their lives helping to save whales or persuading farmers to play classical music to their cows as they got milked. People who wanted an excuse to make it acceptable to take animals into totally unsuitable environments. It was also an insult to anyone who'd gone through many years of tertiary training to earning the title of 'doctor'.

'First session…and *last*…' he heard himself muttering.

'Excuse me…?'

Molly Holmes' echo of his greeting was definitely a query. An outraged one, in fact. She wasn't nearly as tall as Hugh but she seemed to have just grown an inch or two. 'Dr Pryce might have something to say about that. She assured me that all HoDs were on board with the idea. And Christchurch Children's Hospital is now registered as an active participant in an international research trial looking at the benefits of therapy dog visits for paediatric patients.'

'We were on board with *visits*, yes…' Hugh shook off the impression that this woman seemed well spoken. Intelligent. And very defensive…?

'In a ward playroom, perhaps. Or other public areas. Not contaminating an area that needs to be as sterile as possible.'

'We were nowhere near a sterile field while the procedure was happening,' Molly snapped. 'And we follow clear protocols when it comes to hygiene. "Visits", as you call them, are certainly beneficial to sick children but these dogs can make clinical differences in the most distressing situations for children. Procedures like the one Sophie was having today. Or when they're having an anaesthetic induced or they're in Recovery. Or ICU.'

Her words were blurring. 'Recovery?' he echoed. 'ICU? *Theatre…?*'

'Only the induction room. The kind of spaces that parents are also allowed to be in.'

But Hugh held up his hand. 'This is worse than I thought. I don't want to discuss this with you any further, Ms Holmes. No doubt you'll hear more about my concerns from Vivien Pryce in due course.'

'I'll look forward to it,' she said. 'Have a good evening, Mr Ashcroft.' She turned away but then flicked a glance back over her shoulder. 'You might find you'll enjoy it more if you loosen that straitjacket you're wearing first. It might even help you to consider things from a point of view that isn't solely your own.'

Hugh found himself simply standing there, watching the pair of them walk out of the main doors of this hospital.

Shocked…?

Not so much at being told he was so uptight he might have difficulty enjoying his time away from work. He was quite well aware that people considered him to be a workaholic to the point of being antisocial and enough of a recluse for it to be a waste of time inviting him to parties. He didn't care that he might be considered selfish in thinking that his own point of view was the most important, either. It didn't matter to Hugh what they thought of him on a personal level as long as they also considered him to be the top of his field in his chosen specialty.

Which they did.

People weren't normally this rude directly to his face, however.

This was *his* patch. So it was his point of view that carried the weight here.

Any doubt that it would be worth his time and energy to influence the decision the clinical director of this hospital had made in his absence had just been removed.

Maybe Molly Holmes wasn't as intelligent as he'd thought. Did she not realise that smart remark might have just sealed the fate of both herself and her dog?

With a bit of luck, he might never have to set eyes on either of them, ever again.

CHAPTER TWO

DAWN WAS ONLY just breaking as Molly drove her classic 1960 Morris Minor van over the winding road in the hills that bordered the entrance to the city's harbour and the view was enough to make her catch her breath.

'It's going to be a gorgeous day,' she told Oreo. 'Good thing I'm on mornings this week because that means I can take you to the beach after work.'

Molly had moved into the family's much loved holiday house on her return from Australia recently and it was only a short walk to Taylors Mistake beach, which was now Oreo's favourite place to go. Or maybe the real favourite was one of the challenging walking tracks that went for miles through these hills.

No...judging by how excited Oreo was to jump out of the van at the old villa overlooking the harbour where Molly's mother, Jillian, lived, having finally moved off the family farm in the hills, it was the best place in the world to be when she couldn't be at home or with Molly. Of course it was. Molly's mum's young dog, Milo, was Oreo's new best friend and they got to play all day while Molly was at work. Not that she had time to stop and watch the joy with which the dogs greeted each other this morning. An overweight golden retriever was watching the game of chase and roll from the villa's veranda.

'I need to keep going,' Molly told Jillian. 'I want to get in early today.'

The shift handover started at six forty-five a.m. and Molly was always there early. It wasn't simply because this was a new job and she wanted to impress, it was because of her position. As a nurse practitioner, she had spent years in advanced training that gave her a scope of practice well above a registered nurse. Her authority to prescribe medications, interpret laboratory tests, make diagnoses and instigate interventions and treatments meant that she worked closely alongside the consultants and registrars in her area. She was part of every ward round and family meeting, knew every patient under their care and was sometimes the only medical practitioner available on busy days or in an emergency.

It was a position that carried enormous responsibilities and Molly was passionate about doing her job to the very best of her capabilities.

But, okay…there was that bit of extra motivation today.

Because Hugh Ashcroft was back in town and it was only a matter of time until their paths crossed again.

'No worries.' Jillian was fishing in the pocket of her apron for the small treats she always kept there. Oreo and Milo came racing to sit in front of her, being the best-behaved dogs ever.

'See?' she called as Molly was closing the gate behind her. 'Milo's got to do everything Oreo does now. He's going to be another dogtor, I'm sure of it.'

'I'll do some more training with him on my next days off.' Molly nodded. 'See you later, Mum—and thanks so much…'

'You know how much I love providing doggy day care. Hey…how did it go with Oreo yesterday?'

'She was perfect. And the little girl who was having the biopsy just loved her. The surgeon not so much.'

'Oh? Why not?'

'I have a feeling he wasn't expecting to find us there. Or it might be that he's a control freak that would never consider bending a rule.' Molly bit her lip. 'I told him he might need to loosen his straitjacket.'

'Oh, Molly…you *didn't*…'

'Could have been worse.' Molly grinned. 'I could have told him he needed to take the stick out of his bum.'

Her mother laughed and flapped her hand to tell Molly to get going, so she turned to open her driver's door. Her brother had stored the car in a barn in the years she'd been away and the porcelain green shade of paintwork was still perfect. With the sun having risen further and now shining on the vehicle, she realised its olive-green colour was reminding her of something.

Oh…dear Lord…

It was Hugh Ashcroft's eye colour, wasn't it? An unusual shade of green in a human, which was just a bit darker than the traditional colour she'd chosen to repaint the van.

'How did he take that?' Jillian wasn't laughing any longer. 'The surgeon, I mean?'

'I'm not actually quite sure.' But Molly was also unrepentant. He'd deserved to hear that his attitude wasn't appreciated. She shrugged as she pulled the door shut. 'Guess I'm about to find out.'

It was far too early to expect to find the hospital's clinical director in her office but Hugh had sent an email message to her secretary, giving her his timetable for the morning and asking for a meeting to be set up in either her office or his own, with some urgency, but there was no reply by the time he needed to prepare for his first surgery of the day.

Hugh looked into an anaesthetic induction room where an anxious mother was holding a crying toddler. Thirteen-month-old Benji's oral sedative had clearly not been quite strong enough to make what was happening to him tolerable.

'He'll be asleep in just a minute or two, Susan,' he assured the distressed mother. 'Are you okay? Have you thought of anything else you wanted to ask me since I saw you and Benji's father yesterday?'

She shook her head. 'I just want it to be over,' she said. 'Shh…it's okay, Benji. It's not going to hurt.' She cuddled her baby harder as he shrieked in fear and writhed in her arms when the anaesthetist reached towards him with a face mask. 'This part is the hardest…' Susan was losing the battle to hold back her own tears and Hugh could feel himself backing away from the increasing tension and noise level. It was past time he scrubbed in, anyway.

'Try not to worry,' he said briskly. 'We're going to take the very best care of Benji. I'll come and find you as soon as the surgery is finished.'

Matthew was already at the sinks scrubbing his fingers with a sponge. He tilted his head towards the noise coming from the induction room, which was, fortunately, diminishing rapidly.

'Not a happy little camper next door,' he commented.

Hugh's response was a dismissive grunt. He took his watch off and dropped it into the pocket of his scrub tunic. He opened the pack with the soap-impregnated sponge but left it on the ledge while he lathered his arms with soap and used a nail pick. A pre-wash before scrubbing in for the first surgery of the day was mandatory and he rinsed off the soap suds thoroughly before using the sponge to begin a routine that was so familiar and automatic, this could be considered time out. Relaxation, even…

Or maybe not…

'He might have been happier to have that dog in there with him.' Matthew was scrubbing his forearms now. A theatre assistant was hovering nearby with a sterile towel ready. 'That bone biopsy yesterday was quite cool, wasn't it? I've never seen pet therapy used like that before.'

Hugh ignored his registrar's comment this time. He was scrubbing each individual finger now, moving from the little finger to the thumb, a part of his brain quietly counting at least ten strokes on all four anatomical sides of each digit. He had no intention of discussing an issue that had already taken up far too much of his head space. Good grief...his brain had even produced images of that impertinent woman and her scruffy dog as he'd been drifting off to sleep last night.

'So what can you tell me about our first case?'

Matthew dropped his towel and pushed his arms into the sterile gown the assistant was holding for him. 'Benji's parents noticed a bump on his collarbone when he was about four months old. It's got steadily more prominent and imaging has revealed a congenital pseudoarthrosis of the clavicle.'

'Which is?'

'A "false joint". Where a single bone, such as a clavicle or tibia, grows as two bones.'

'Cause?'

'Most likely due to a birth injury.'

'And why is it an issue?'

'The bump can become pronounced enough to be unsightly but, more importantly, it can cause pain and affect the function of the shoulder, which is what's happening in Benji's case. He's developed an odd crawling style because he's avoiding using his right arm.'

Hugh nodded. He was holding his arms under the stream of water from the tap now, letting suds run off from his fingers towards his elbows. 'And what are we going to do?'

'An open debridement of the bone ends and

then fixation with clavicle plates and, if necessary, a bone graft with cancellous bone harvested from the iliac crest to fill the gap.'

'Good.' Hugh took the sterile towel from the tongs held by the theatre assistant and dried his hands carefully. 'I'll leave you to stay and see how they apply a wrap-around body and arm cast when the surgery's completed. I'll be popping down to my office on the ward for a meeting with Vivien Pryce before we get started on our second case for this morning.' He turned to put his arms through the sleeves of his gown. 'It shouldn't take long. I expect I'll be back by the time young Benji has gone through to Recovery.'

Baby Chloe giggled as Molly used a fluffy soft toy to tickle her tummy.

'What a gorgeous smile. She doesn't seem that bothered by having her legs strung up in the air like this, does she? We'll see how she goes today now that the weight on the traction's been increased.'

'I hope I can still breastfeed her.'

'It's possible. Not easy but if you can wriggle under the strings and lie sideways beside her, she'll be able to latch on. I've seen mums do it.' She smiled at Chloe's mother. 'It's amazing how you can find a way to do the things that are really important. I love that you're not giving up on the breastfeeding.'

The traction mechanism attached to each end of the cot was gradually stretching ligaments to try and position a congenitally dislocated hip so that it could then be held in the correct place by a splint for months to come.

'She's going to need surgery if the traction doesn't work, isn't she? That's why we're in this ward?'

'It's certainly a possibility.' Molly checked the baby's case notes. 'She's due for an X-ray tomorrow so we should have a better idea of how things are going after that. Would you like me to get the surgeon to come and have a chat to you before then?'

'Yes, please… I always try and hope for the best but being prepared for the worst is kind of an insurance policy, isn't it?'

'I couldn't agree more.' Molly was writing on Chloe's chart. 'I've finished my ward round so I'm going to go and leave a note for the surgeon to come and see you as soon as possible.' She flicked a page over. 'Oh…' An odd knot suddenly formed in her stomach. 'Chloe was admitted under Mr Ashcroft's team, yes?'

'Yes. I haven't met him yet, though—only his registrar. They told me he was away doing a lecture tour in America but he'd be back in time if Chloe did end up needing an operation.'

'He's back now. I met him for the first time myself yesterday.'

'What's he like? He must be very good at his job if he's asked to give international talks.'

Molly swerved the question by making a sound that could have been agreement. Or perhaps it was encouragement, as she picked up the fluffy toy to try and make Chloe giggle again.

The delicious sound of a happy baby stayed with Molly as she scribbled a note to ask Hugh Ashcroft to visit his potential patient's mother. She could have left it with the ward manager to deliver or put it in the departmental pigeonholes for mail but she was due for a break and wanted a breath of fresh air. Heading for the access to the courtyard garden that opened off the foyer area just outside the ward entrance took her very close to the consultants' offices, so she decided to put it on his desk herself. That way, she could make sure he saw it immediately.

She opened the door without waiting for a response to her polite knock because she knew he was upstairs in Theatre with a full list for the day. The shock of seeing him standing behind his desk peering at his computer screen was enough to make her jaw drop.

'Oh, my god,' she said. 'You're not supposed to be here.'

'It's *you*...' It was a statement rather than a question but he was looking as startled as she was. 'I could say the same thing,' he added, slowly. 'You're certainly not supposed to be in *my* office.'

He was staring at the scrubs she was wearing. At her hair, which, admittedly, was probably already trying to escape the clips she used to try and tame it during work hours. His eyebrows rose as his gaze flicked down to the stethoscope hanging around her neck and the lanyard that made it obvious she was a staff member. And then that gaze shifted again, to look straight at her. 'Who the hell *are* you?'

Oh...the intensity in those olive-green eyes that could be due to either suspicion or anger was...well, it was disconcerting to say the least. It had to be nerves that were pinching deep in Molly's gut right now because she knew what was coming—a well-deserved bollocking for having been so rude to a consultant surgeon yesterday?

'My name's Molly Holmes.' She lifted her chin. 'I started work here as a nurse practitioner last week.'

'But...what were you doing here yesterday? With that dog?'

'I've been involved in pet therapy for years. It's what I do on my days off.'

There was a moment's silence during which Molly noticed something was changing in that gaze she was pinned by. Was it softening? Because Hugh Ashcroft was now seeing her as a colleague and not a layperson who volunteered to bring her pet dog into a hospital occasionally? Or could he be just a little impressed that she chose to spend her days off in the same place she worked? That she cared enough about her patients to be here when she wasn't being paid to do so?

Perhaps being impressed was a bit much to expect.

But he wasn't looking angry so much. He was looking…

Puzzled…? Or curious? As if interest might be winning a battle with irritation…?

Her nervousness was receding now that it didn't feel like she was in quite so much trouble with one of her senior colleagues but, strangely, that sensation in Molly's gut wasn't going away. If anything, it seemed to have become even stronger.

He knew he was staring.

He knew it was a rude thing to do, but Hugh couldn't help himself. It almost felt as if, by keeping a steady gaze on this woman, he might be able to find his balance.

It wasn't often that something knocked him sideways but having Molly Holmes walk into his office like that had done it. He'd left the hospital yesterday quite confident that he would never see her—or her dog—again but…here she was. In his work space. His *happy* space. Not only that, she was a nurse practitioner. Someone who was highly trained enough to be filling gaps and monitoring his patients, possibly better than his more junior registrars.

Someone that he would expect to have a close working relationship with.

Vivien Pryce, the clinical director, who was going to arrive in his office at any moment, according to the email he'd just read, might not be very happy if Hugh said everything he'd been planning to say to her about yesterday's incident with the dog in his procedure room.

Hugh cleared his throat.

'About yesterday…' he began. 'About your dog…'

And then he stopped because he couldn't think of what to say next.

He was still staring. At her brown eyes that were fringed with lashes as dark as her hair. Her skin was tanned enough to make him think she spent a lot of time outdoors and…

…and she was smiling at him.

'Oreo,' she supplied to fill in the gap. 'She liked you, Mr Ashcroft.' Her eyebrows lifted as if she had found this quite surprising. 'And I have to admit that my dog is usually a very good judge of character.'

Hugh remembered the way the dog had been looking up at him yesterday and waving its tail in approval. Smiling at him… He actually shook his head to get rid of the image of those brown eyes, as warm as melted chocolate, fixed on him. Not unlike Molly's eyes, come to think of it.

The list of objections he had been more than ready to discuss with Vivien seemed to be getting less defined. Hugh found himself frowning as he tried to focus.

'It wasn't that I didn't know a pet therapy programme was being considered for our ward,' he said, a little curtly. 'But nobody said anything about allowing animals to have access to the kind of areas you mentioned, like an intensive care unit. Or a procedure room, for that matter. I was…surprised, to say the least.'

Molly was nodding. 'I'm sorry about that. And I take full responsibility. There was a meeting last week, while you were still away, and because I've already been involved with a similar programme in Australia I was invited to bring

Oreo in. It was only going to be an orientation but then Radiology let us know about Sophie's appointment and Vivien asked if we could visit and it just sort of grew from there. Sophie fell in love with Oreo and asked if she could go with her for the biopsy and I said she'd love to if she was allowed and…' Molly finally paused for breath. 'Anyway… I do apologise. I can try to ensure that everyone's aware she's going to be present next time.'

Next time…? I don't think so…

Hugh wasn't aware his thought had been audible until he saw Molly's expression change. Until he saw the fierce gleam in her eyes that told him she was quite prepared to fight for whatever she was passionate about.

'There are some articles you might like to read when you have a spare moment,' she said. 'There aren't too many peer-reviewed studies that have been written up yet but anecdotal evidence is gaining quite a following. The trial that Dr Pryce has enrolled us in will be hoping to reproduce the kind of results being seen overseas, where people are reporting quite dramatic improvements in parameters like anxiety levels and pain scales in children who have animal companions in stressful medical situations. Measurable results with blood pressures and heart rates dropping, which is a pretty good indication that pain or stress levels are diminishing—'

The knock on the door interrupted her and Hugh saw her eyes widen when Vivien Pryce entered his office. He also saw the flash of something that looked very much like fear and…

…and he suddenly felt guilty because he could have caused Molly some serious problems that might have ruined the start of her new job if he'd gone ahead with his complaints.

He also felt quite strongly, and very oddly, as if he wanted to protect her, which was both very unexpected and just as unwelcome.

Oh, no…

Molly saw the apologetic expression on the clinical director's face as she entered Hugh Ashcroft's office.

'Sorry, Hugh. I've been putting out fires so far all morning and I've only got a minute or two now but my secretary said it sounded like you wanted to talk to me about something urgent.' Her sideways glance was curious. 'Is it about our first dogtor consultation yesterday? Is that why Molly's here, too?'

'No…' Molly edged towards the door. 'I just came to leave a note for Mr Ashcroft.' She hurriedly put the now rather crumpled piece of paper, asking Hugh to go and talk to Chloe's mother, on the edge of the desk. 'I'll leave you to it.'

'Don't go.' Hugh's tone sounded like a command. 'You probably need to know what I was about to say to Vivien, anyway.'

Molly bit her lip. If he wasn't about to tell Vivien how inappropriate he considered it to be to have animals in a procedure room, he was intending to tell her that their new nurse practitioner was lacking the kind of respect a senior consultant surgeon was entitled to expect.

She had to agree that he should be able to expect some privacy in his own office without having people barging in uninvited. And he certainly shouldn't have been told that he was so buttoned up he couldn't bend far enough to consider that the opinions of others might actually be as valid as his own.

But Hugh was nodding at Vivien as Molly held her breath. 'That was, in fact, what we've just been discussing,' he said. 'I was explaining that I wasn't aware there was any mention of allowing animals in areas that most clinicians wouldn't consider to be remotely suitable for pet therapy when we had that initial departmental meeting on the subject.'

'That is true. Personally, I wasn't aware of the most recent literature concerning the therapeutic benefits of allowing dogs in those kinds of areas until I was having a chat to Molly after her job application interview. It was, admittedly, an addition that should have been more widely discussed before we put it into action.'

The sound Hugh made was a cross between agreement and annoyance. Then he shrugged. 'Perhaps it's not too late. You might like to send me the links to those papers when you have a spare moment.'

Vivien flicked another glance in Molly's direction. There was curiosity in that lightning-fast glance as well—as if she was surprised that Molly had somehow defused the bomb that had been about to be hurled?

'I'll do that. But if it's more information you need, Hugh, it's Molly you should talk to. She's got far more experience in this field than anyone here. I'll also forward the memo I got from the research technician who was recording vital sign measurements on Sophie yesterday. If you compare them with the control case we monitored last week, you can see a rather startling difference. I know it's early days but I think this is going to be a very exciting trial to be part of.' She was smiling at Molly now. 'And we have our recently appointed nurse practitioner to thank for getting it off the ground.'

Hugh might have resisted the opportunity to get Molly into trouble but he wasn't about to go as far as being friendly to his new colleague. He was reaching to pick up the note Molly had put on his desk and he scanned it swiftly. 'Tell them I'll be on the ward as soon as my surgery list is complete for the day,' he said. 'That should be around four o'clock if we have no emergencies or complications to deal with. And if I'm not holding everyone up by having unscheduled meetings.' He glanced up at the clock on his wall. 'Which means I need to be scrubbed in again in less than five minutes.'

His nod signalled the end of this unscheduled meeting with Molly. He moved towards the door and Vivien turned to follow him out.

'Keep me posted on Sophie's case, would you, please, Hugh? I was thinking about how hard this is going to be for her family last night. Did you know she's the star of her ballet class? Her dad just put up a rail in her bedroom to be a barre for her to practise with.'

It was no surprise that this aloof surgeon ignored such a personal detail. Molly could hear the clinical detachment in his voice as he walked away with Vivien. 'She's scheduled for a PET scan about now. I'll forward the results…'

Molly headed back to pass on the message for Chloe's mother. The handover for the afternoon shift would be over long before Hugh was due to be back on the ward so it was very unlikely that she would see him again today, which would probably be a relief as far as Mr Ashcroft was concerned.

It was a relief for Molly as well because she was quite sure that she had, somehow, dodged a bullet.

There was no reason at all to feel disappointed. Molly had a busy few hours ahead of her dealing with whatever challenges arose in a surgical paediatric ward. Her pager was beeping right now, in fact, to alert her to a potentially urgent situation.

Moments later, she was on her way to replace an IV line that a toddler had managed to pull out. She could hear the two-year-old boy's screams already as she sped down the corridor. This could keep her occupied for quite some time but it was just the kind of challenge she enjoyed the most— winning the confidence of a terrified child and succeeding in a necessary intervention with the least amount of trauma. It was a shame she didn't have Oreo here to help, mind you.

But, by four o'clock, she would be back at her own mother's house to collect her beloved canine companion. She'd do some training with Milo before she went home but the days were lengthening nicely now that summer wasn't far away. There would be time for a walk on the beach with Oreo before it got dark.

Feeling disappointed that she wouldn't be seeing Hugh Ashcroft again today was…

…weird. That was what it was.

CHAPTER THREE

SUNSET WASN'T FAR off but there was still enough time to go and play on the beach, especially when they only had to go through the gate at the bottom of the garden and run along the track through the marram grass on the sand dunes to get past the driftwood and near the waves, where there was enough space to throw the frisbee.

Molly kicked off her sandals and got close enough for the last wash of the waves to cover her feet. She flicked the frisbee and laughed as Oreo hurled herself into the chase with a bark of delight and then leapt into the air to catch the plastic saucer and bring it back to drop at her feet. This time with her dog was a world away from the stress that could come from her work and completely different from the focus that came from the training sessions she did with Oreo and now Milo on a daily basis. It was simply hanging out. Loving each other's company.

Pure fun.

She wasn't the only person taking advantage

of the last of the sun's rays to have some fun. A lone surfer, protected by a full body wetsuit, was well out to sea, waiting for a bigger wave.

For a disquieting moment, Molly was taken back in time. She was a teenager in love for the first time, watching her boyfriend and her brother out catching waves on a summer evening, and she'd never been so happy. The pain—and shock—of her first romantic disaster when she was dumped a few months later had never been forgotten.

On the positive side, the pain was never *quite* that life-shatteringly bad when it happened again.

On the negative side, it had happened too often.

Okay…sometimes it had been her decision to call time on a relationship that wasn't going anywhere but, more often, it hadn't been her choice. It was usually an amicable ending because they were great friends but, quite understandably, the guys moved on because they wanted something more in a life partner. And sometimes, it came too close to an echo of that first heartbreak.

Molly had given up trying to work out why she always seemed to be put in the 'friend zone'. The men she liked didn't seem bothered that she wasn't blonde and blue-eyed. Or that she had the solid, healthy kind of body that suited a girl from the farm. It certainly wasn't that she wasn't good company or intelligent enough to be able to have an interesting conversation.

She told herself for years that she just hadn't met the right person. That she'd know when she did and she wasn't going to settle for less. That she might be surprised to find him around the very next corner in her life. But the last break-up—the one that had persuaded Molly it was time to go home to New Zealand—was taking a bit longer to get over.

Getting settled again and starting a new job were good excuses to have no interest in even looking for male companionship but, to be honest, Molly was almost ready to embrace single-dom. If she wasn't looking, maybe the 'one' would come around that corner and find her. If he didn't, it wouldn't be the end of the world. It wasn't as if she were alone, after all. She bent to pick up the frisbee Oreo had dropped hopefully in front of her and threw it again.

Oreo's joyful bark as she chased after the toy made her smile.

This was the kind of happy she could trust to last…

When she straightened up, she saw the surfer catch the wave he'd been waiting for and when he leapt to his feet, Molly found herself slowing to watch him. She didn't even notice the frisbee being dropped within easy reach.

Wow...

This guy was seriously good at surfing. Molly liked to swim in the sea but she'd never got bitten by the surfing bug. Her older brother had, though—which was how she'd met her first boyfriend—and she'd heard and seen enough over her teenage years to know how much effort and skill went into making it look this easy. This graceful.

Right from the moment he got to his feet, he was in control and there was no way Molly could look away before he reached the end of this wave. To be able to sense the power and purpose in his movement from this far away was something special. This person was passionate about what they were doing—totally oblivious to any audience, living in the moment and loving it.

He had done an aerial move within seconds, flipping his board into the air above the lip of the wave and then landing to twist and turn along the wave face. As the height and strength of the wave collapsed he even did a flashy re-entry turn off the end of it. And then he dropped down to lie on his board and paddle back out to sea, as if he couldn't wait to catch another wave. As if his life depended on it, even...

Oreo's bark made Molly realise she had ignored the frisbee for too long and she turned her attention back to the game, but as she reached the end of the beach and turned back towards home she caught sight of the surfer again—now a dark blob against the increasing colour in the sky behind him, reflecting the sunset happening on the other side of the hills. He wasn't showing off this time. He was simply poised on his board, at one with the limitless ocean he'd just been flirting with, as he rode the wave right to the wash of shallow foam so close to the beach he could step off and be only ankle deep. He picked his board up at that point, slung it under his arm and walked out of the sea…straight towards Molly.

Oreo was normally wary of strangers and stayed protectively close, often touching her legs, so Molly was astonished to see her take off and run towards the surfer. When she got close, she dropped her frisbee and then put her nose down on her paws and her bum in the air to invite the man to play. When he walked straight past her, she looked confused for a moment but then grabbed the toy and ran after the man. This time she got right in front of him before she dropped it. Molly increased her pace, ready to apologise for the annoyance her dog was creating.

But then she stopped dead in her tracks, completely lost for words.

Blindsided…

Never, in a million years, would she have guessed that the man whose longstanding passion for what he was doing on the waves showed in his level of skill and every confident, graceful movement of his body could possibly be someone who could also be so lacking in an emotional connection to other living creatures that he couldn't embrace the pure joy of being able to provide comfort to a small, scared child.

Did Hugh Ashcroft have an identical twin?

Or had she stumbled into the private life of a person who was actually the opposite of who he appeared to be in the company of others?

How—and *why*—could someone be like that?

Curiosity was quite a powerful emotion, wasn't it?

'Hullo, Molly.'

So, there was definitely no identical twin, then.

'Hullo, Mr Ashcroft...'

Even a tiny shake of his head released droplets of sea water from his hair. Hair that was very neatly cut but was so wet and full of salt, it was spiky, so even his hairstyle was utterly different.

'Call me Hugh, for heaven's sake,' he said. 'There's no need to be so formal, at work *or* away from it.'

He was staring at her, but this was very different from how it had felt when he'd given her a look of this intensity at work, when he'd demanded to know who the hell she was. He wasn't wearing his surgical scrubs, he was encased in skintight neoprene that was almost as sexy as seeing him wearing nothing at all. And he was dripping wet.

Okay…maybe it did feel pretty much the same. Because Molly could feel that curl of sensation unfolding in her gut, not unlike one of the large waves still breaking offshore, and, this time, she knew it had nothing to do with being nervous.

It didn't have anything to do with her confusion, either, although the burning question of which person was the *real* Hugh Ashcroft wasn't about to go away.

No. This was something else entirely. Something even more powerful than that curiosity.

It had everything to do with…attraction.

Sexual attraction…

Dear Lord…she had the hots for someone she was going to be working with? Someone who had made no secret of his disapproval of her taking her dog into sacrosanct areas of the hospital. Who'd even looked vaguely disgusted when he'd caught her shedding a tear?

'Fine…' Molly was pleased to manage to sound so offhand. 'Hugh it is.'

She reached down to pick up the frisbee and flicked it towards the sea. Oreo bounced through the shallow water to catch it before it hit the waves.

'I've forgotten your dog's name,' Hugh said.

He was moving again, towards where a towel had been left on the sand, neatly rolled up.

'Oreo.'

'Like the cookie? Of course…he's black and white. Great name.'

'*She*… Oreo's a girl.'

The correction sounded like a reprimand but Hugh ignored it. He wasn't really interested in her dog, was he? Or her? And that was just as well. It meant that Molly could dismiss that moment of inappropriate attraction and make sure it didn't happen again.

Oreo was back with the frisbee. Molly held out her hand but Oreo dropped it right beside Hugh's bare foot. He bent down but didn't pick up the toy. Instead, he picked up the towel and started walking again, towards the car parking area that also had a facility block.

'I'd better get a shower before I get too cold,' he said. The glance over his shoulder felt like a question.

'I'm heading that way myself.' She nodded. Oreo picked up the frisbee and followed them.

'I can only see my car,' Hugh said, a few steps later. 'Where did you park?'

'I live here,' Molly told him. 'See that little white cottage with the red roof and the big chimney up on the road?'

'You live right by the beach? Lucky you…'

'It's not exactly my house. It's the family bach. I grew up on a farm and this was where we came for holidays.'

'You still count as a local, then. I've always wondered how it got its name. Someone told me that there was a shipwreck here and that was the mistake.'

Molly laughed. 'I think getting the ship stuck on the beach was the second mistake that Captain Taylor made. The first one was thinking he was going into the harbour in Lyttleton, I believe. It was back in the early settler days of the eighteen-fifties.'

Good grief…did she think Hugh might want a history lesson? Molly didn't dare look at him. She glanced sideways at the waves, instead.

'My older brother, Jack, got into surfing when he was just a kid and was going to competitions by the time he was a teenager.' She bit her lip. 'Don't think he's as good as you are, though.'

The sudden silence made her look back to find Hugh blinking as if he was startled by the compliment but then he turned to look at the waves again himself. 'Did you surf, too?'

'No. It's always been about animals for me. I rode horses and did dog trials—you know? Rounding up sheep and getting them into a pen?'

Oreo was walking beside them, clearly resigned to the fact that the frisbee game was over for the day. Curiously, she was walking beside Hugh rather than Molly.

'I think you've got an admirer.'

'Excuse me?'

Oh, help…did he think she meant herself, after she'd told him how good he was at surfing? She tilted her head and he glanced down to follow her line of sight. Oreo looked up at him and waved her tail.

It was Hugh who broke a still awkward silence.

'Vivien sent me those articles,' he said. 'I had time to browse one of them when I went back to the ward to talk to Chloe's mother this afternoon.'

'Oh…?'

'I didn't realise quite how extensive the range of therapies is that animals can be involved with. Like physiotherapy.'

Molly nodded. The turnoff for the track up to her house wasn't far ahead of them but she didn't want this conversation to end quite yet. Not when she could talk about something that might make a real difference to how enjoyable her new job was going to be.

'I love working with physios. It's amazing how reaching out to pat a dog or taking one for a walk, even if it's just to the door of their room and back, can get them past the pain barrier of starting to move again after surgery. Oreo's good at pretending to take medicine with kids, too. She'll drink liquid from a syringe or take a "pill" that's actually one of her treats. And it's not just beneficial to the patients. Most staff members love having a dog around and the parents and siblings of patients can get a lot of comfort out of it...' Molly sucked in a breath. She had too much she wanted to say and not enough time. 'What could be better for anyone who's having a tough time than to be able to cuddle a dog?'

'I wouldn't know.'

But Hugh's response sounded merely polite. He was looking past Molly, towards the house she'd pointed out as being where she lived. She knew he would be able to see the track leading away from the beach and, if she kept walking with him, it would be obvious that she was doing it for a reason and not simply because they were going in the same direction. Heaven forbid that it might occur to him that she'd had even a moment of being interested in him as anything other than a colleague.

'See you tomorrow, Hugh.' Molly turned away. A glance was all it took for Oreo to follow her.

'Have a good evening, Molly.'

Hugh's farewell was an echo of what she'd said to him—good heavens, was it only yesterday? Just before she told him that he might like to loosen his straitjacket. In retrospect, after seeing the way he'd moved his body in response to the force of the waves, it had been an astonishingly unfounded accusation to make. Worse, remembering what it was like watching him reminded Molly of her physical reaction to having him standing in front of her, dripping wet, in that skin-tight wetsuit. She was actually feeling that twist of sensation in her gut all over again.

And that was disturbing enough for Molly to avoid looking back at him at all costs as she walked away.

Oreo looked back, though. And when she looked up at Molly again, it felt like her dog was asking the same question that was filling her own head.

'I don't know,' she heard herself saying aloud. 'We'll just have to wait and see, won't we?'

The meeting room was full of people.

There were representatives from the paediatric oncology, radiology and surgical departments. The head of physiotherapy was here, the ward manager, Lizzie, a senior pharmacist, a senior nurse specialist and the nurse practitioner, Molly, and a child psychologist and family counsellor.

Oh, yeah...and one dog. It must be one of Molly's days off. She had probably been intending to bring Oreo into the hospital anyway but, oddly, it felt quite appropriate that the dog and her owner who'd been there at the beginning of this case were also present at such an important family meeting. Oreo was lying very still, her nose on her paws, on the floor beside Molly's foot.

It was very quiet.

Quiet enough to hear Sophie Jacobs' mother, Joanne, pull in a shaky breath, as if she was trying to control the urge to cry. Her husband, Simon, was staring at the ceiling and it was possible to see the muscles in his jaw working to keep it clenched. He was also trying not to cry in public, wasn't he? Sophie's grandmother had also been included in this meeting to discuss the diagnosis, ongoing treatment and prognosis for their precious seven-year-old girl and she had a wadded tissue pressed beneath one eye.

Hugh glanced at the paediatric oncology consultant who, along with the paediatrician who had been the admitting physician, had delivered the results of all the tests they had done and confirmed the devastating news that Sophie did, indeed, have a malignant osteosarcoma. He'd provided details of the staging process and prognosis that had, no doubt, been too much to understand at this point and would need to be talked about again, probably more than once.

The oncologist had also explained her role to care for Sophie as she received an intensive period of neoadjuvant or pre-operative chemotherapy before the surgery to remove the tumour.

The pharmacist had finished an outline of the kind of drugs that would be used for the chemotherapy and answered questions about how side effects such as nausea and hair loss might be managed. The family had been warned early on in the investigations that if the tumour was malignant then amputation, rather than any limb-saving surgery, would very likely be necessary.

The oncologist met Hugh's glance and gave a discreet nod. It was the right time for him to say something about the upcoming surgery for Sophie.

There was a screen at this end of the room and Hugh tapped the mouse pad on his laptop to bring up an image.

'This was the very first X-ray we took of Sophie's leg,' he said quietly. 'And it was immediately obvious that she had something significant going on at the distal end of her femur—almost directly on top of the knee joint. We have a lot more information now, thanks to the biopsy, MRI, the PET and CT scans and all the other tests that Sophie has very bravely put up with over the last week or two.'

Joanne blew her nose. 'Thanks to Oreo,' she said. She smiled across the table at Molly. 'I don't know how we could have coped without you.'

'It's been our pleasure,' Molly said. 'I'm going to take Oreo to visit her again in a few minutes, to let you have more time to talk to everybody today. I just wanted you to know that we consider ourselves to be part of this team and we'll be here whenever I have my days off.'

Sophie's father simply nodded brusquely.

'The good news—even though it might not seem like that at the moment—is that this is a primary osteosarcoma and not evidence of metastatic disease from somewhere else. Even better, the PET scan, amongst the other tests, has shown us that the clinical stage is early and the tumour is still intracompartmental, which means that it hasn't extended as far as the periosteum, which is the membrane of blood vessels and nerves that wraps around the bone.' Hugh was putting up images from the scans now. 'The lymph nodes are clear and there's no sign of any hot spots at all in the lungs or any other bones, which are the most likely targets for metastases. This is all really good news because it gives us confidence that the cancer hasn't spread. At all…'

Hugh paused for a moment to let that positive statement sink in. He saw the glances exchanged between Sophie's parents and, if he let himself, he knew he would be able to feel the beat of hope in the room. Not that he was going to indulge in sharing anything close to joy when he still had the hardest part of this meeting to get through.

'We still need to treat this cancer aggressively

enough to try and ensure we get rid of it completely and it can't recur—or spread—and that
means that the surgery Sophie is going to need
will be amputation. The procedure that we will
be recommending is the one I mentioned to you
as a possibility the other day—the rotationplasty
salvage procedure.'

'*No...*' Joanne pressed her hand to her mouth
to stifle a distressed cry and her husband put his
arms around her.

Hugh clicked onto a new image but as he
shifted his gaze he caught the way Molly had
dropped her hand to Oreo's head—as if she
needed a bit of comfort herself? He could understand that the concept was confronting but it
was, without doubt, the best option for Sophie.

'As I explained, what happens is that the bottom
of the femur—where the tumour is located—the
whole knee joint and the upper tibia are surgi-
cally removed, with the cancer and a wide clear
margin around it also removed. The lower leg is
then rotated one hundred and eighty degrees and
attached to the femur.'

Hugh could see that Joanne Jacobs still hadn't
glanced up at the image on the screen of a young
boy who'd had this procedure. With no prosthesis
on, he had the unusual appearance on one leg of
a foot pointing backwards at knee level.

'Because the foot is on backwards, it can function as a knee joint,' he continued calmly. 'A special prosthesis is made that the foot fits into and it provides much greater mobility and stability than a full leg amputation would. It also lowers the risk of phantom leg pain.'

He put up a new image of the boy with the foot hidden inside his artificial lower leg and perhaps Sophie's father had murmured some encouragement to his wife because Joanne finally looked up as well. The next image was of the boy kicking a football—a wide grin on his face.

'The bone will continue to grow as you would expect in a young child and, of course, the prosthesis will be adjusted to fit.' Hugh closed his laptop. 'Younger children have another real advantage in that their brains learn more easily to use their ankle as a knee and adapt their walking patterns.'

The physiotherapist at the meeting was nodding. 'I can answer any questions when you're ready to talk about it,' she said.

Joanne shook her head. She wasn't ready. She folded herself further into her husband's arms and it was obvious she was sobbing silently by the way her shoulders were shaking.

There was no point in trying to reassure these distressed parents any further at this time. Hugh caught the counsellor's gaze with a raised eyebrow and the silent communication suggested that she would stay here a little longer but, yes, it would be better for everyone else to leave and give this couple some private time to deal with their initial reactions. Others had seen the silent message and, as a group, they were beginning to leave the room.

Hugh picked up his laptop as he saw Molly and Oreo leaving. He wanted to catch a moment of the oncology consultant's time for a chat about the chemotherapy regime that would be started for Sophie, hopefully today. He had cleared a good space of time this afternoon so he would check back to see if Sophie's parents wanted to talk to him about anything, but he suspected he might be the last person they'd want to see again today.

When he walked back past the meeting room, Joanne and Simon were nowhere to be seen and the psychologist was shutting the door behind her.

'I suggested they went for a walk outside and got some fresh air before they went to see Sophie so that she wouldn't see how upset they were,' she told Hugh. 'But we've made a plan to discuss how and when to talk to her about the amputation. I'm going to see if I can set up a meeting with the parents of that boy in your photos. I know they'll be happy to offer their support and it could be a game-changer for everybody. He's a few years older than Sophie now but maybe he'd be up for coming in to visit and show her his leg?'

'Good idea.' But Hugh's response was brisk. Everyone involved on the team assigned to this case had different roles and thank goodness there were people who were more than willing to immerse themselves in the social, psychological and emotional side of a life-changing diagnosis like the one Sophie Jacobs had just received. His job was to make sure he gave her the best chance of, not only survival by completely removing the tumour, but the best quality of life possible, going forward, by advocating for a procedure he knew was the best option. His role was all about the surgery and the most important part of his role would be inside an operating theatre with a patient who was sound asleep and any emotional family members completely out of sight—and mind.

Just being in the tense atmosphere of that family meeting had been enough for Hugh to be hanging out for a bit of private time for himself to prepare for the rest of his day. He didn't need a walk in any fresh air, though. The peace and quiet of his office with the door firmly closed would be quite good enough and the close proximity of that small, personal space was too tempting to resist.

Between the paediatric orthopaedic surgical

ward and the row of consultants' offices was a courtyard roof garden, opening off the foyer space that housed the stairway and bank of lifts. It wasn't huge but it provided the nice aesthetic of an open space with some lush greenery and seating. The concrete pavers were smooth enough to make it easy for IV poles to be pushed or beds to be rolled outside for a bit of sunshine.

As Hugh walked past the floor to ceiling windows to get to his office, he saw a wheelchair parked to one side of the central square of pavers. And then he saw that it was Sophie Jacobs who was sitting in that wheelchair. The wide door to the garden hadn't been completely closed so he could hear music that was being played outside. An old tune he remembered from high school discos back in the day—Abba's 'Dancing Queen'.

Sophie had a huge grin on her face and her arms were in the air as if she were dancing to the music, but she wasn't alone. Both Molly and Oreo were out there with her.

Hugh's steps slowed and then stopped. What on earth were they doing?

Skipping…that was what it was.

But it wasn't just Molly skipping. Oreo was holding up one front paw as she hopped and then the other. And then Molly made a hand signal and Oreo stood on her hind legs and went around in a circle.

Molly turned in a circle as well and Sophie clapped her hands.

Then Molly started moving in a diagonal line across the square, straight towards where Hugh was standing, but she didn't notice him. She was watching Oreo as she took long steps, her legs very slightly bent, which seemed to be a signal to the dog to go in figures of eight, her own gaze fixed on Molly's as she was weaving through the space between her legs from one side and then the other.

It was only when dog and owner paused a beat before they started skipping again in the opposite direction and he realised that it was in time to the music that Hugh remembered Molly telling her that Oreo loved to dance.

This was what she and her dog were doing, wasn't it?

Dancing...

And obviously loving doing it as much as Sophie was loving watching it.

It was kind of cute, Hugh conceded.

But it was also...

Mesmerising?

His feet were certainly glued to the floor. His gaze was glued to Molly. To the changing expressions on her face and her hand gestures that were a language all of their own and the lithe movements of her body as she bent and twisted, reached and curled.

It was…

Okay…it was damned sexy, *that* was what it actually was.

Hugh could feel his body waking up, as fixated as his gaze had been on this woman and what she was doing. He could feel tendrils of a sensation that was both physical and mental and, while he might not have felt it to quite this degree since he was an adolescent, he knew exactly what it was.

Attraction…

Desire…?

A want that was powerful enough to feel like a need.

And the shock of that recognition was more than enough to break the spell that Hugh Ashcroft had fallen under. He could move his feet again and that was exactly what he did to escape from the disturbing realisation that he was sexually attracted to the new nurse practitioner.

Not that it was a problem. Hugh was more than capable of both keeping his own feelings completely private and making sure that something professionally awkward simply wouldn't be allowed to reappear.

But he did need the privacy and time out of his own office for a few minutes even more now than he had a few minutes ago.

CHAPTER FOUR

'I CAN'T SEE this working.' The older woman watching what Molly was doing with a young patient and his mother was shaking her head. 'It's never going to stay properly clean, is it?'

'Don't be so negative, Mum. That's why I'm getting as much practice in as I can before we take Benji home this afternoon.'

'I know it's going to be a bit of a challenge at times,' Molly conceded. 'Especially in the first week or two.' She offered the anxious grandmother a smile. 'I'm sure your help is going to be very much appreciated, Louise, but Susan is a very competent mother and I know she's going to cope brilliantly. Look at how well she's doing this nappy change.'

Susan's baby, Benji, was in an unwieldy plaster cast that wrapped around his chest and one arm to keep it completely still after the surgery he'd had to remove the false joint on his clavicle. He was also coping well with the nappy change, waving his unrestrained arm in the air, trying to grab his mother's necklace as she leaned over him.

'You're doing a great job,' Molly said. 'Tuck the edges of the first nappy right under the cast and then we'll put another one on top. We want to avoid the cast getting wet or dirty if at all possible. You may find it easier to use a smaller size than usual for the first nappy.'

'What do I do if it does get dirty or wet?'

'Use just a damp washcloth to clean it. If it's really damp, you can use a hairdryer on a cool setting to speed up the drying process or take Benji outside to get a bit of sunshine on it. Another good tip is to use a towel as a big bib when he's got food or a drink in his hands.'

'He must weigh twice as much with that cast on.' Louise sighed.

'He'll certainly be top heavy and won't be able to sit up by himself,' Molly agreed. 'He'll need to be propped up with pillows and cushions and don't let him try and walk by himself. The last thing you want is a fall, so he'll need to be carried everywhere.'

Louise made a tutting sound. 'You're going to have to be careful when you pick him up, Susie. You'll be in trouble if you put your back out again.' She turned to Molly. 'How long is he going to be in this cast?'

Molly opened her mouth to answer but stopped

as she saw Benji's surgeon coming through the door of the room. Hugh Ashcroft was wearing scrubs and still had a mask dangling by its strings around his neck. Had he left his registrar to finish up in Theatre after the actual surgery was completed and ducked down to the ward for some urgent task?

Hugh acknowledged Molly with a brisk nod but his gaze went straight to Susan.

'Benji's discharge papers are signed,' he told her. 'I've reviewed the X-ray he had taken yesterday and I'm happy that he doesn't need to stay in any longer. The clavicle is exactly where it needs to be and it should heal very fast.' He shifted his gaze to Benji's grandmother. 'In answer to your question, this cast will need to stay on for five to six weeks. We'll see Benji well before then, however, and monitor his progress in our outpatient clinic.' He was turning to leave. 'You'll find a phone number on the discharge information to call if there are any problems, so please get in touch with the team if you have anything you're worried about.'

'Thank you ever so much for everything you've done, Mr Ashcroft,' Susan said.

'Ashcroft…' Louise was staring. 'You're not Claire Ashcroft's boy, are you?'

'Ah…' Hugh had taken a step towards the door. 'Claire was my mother's name, yes…'

'You probably don't remember me. I used to work for the same house cleaning company as your mother. Spick and Span? Goodness, it must be more than twenty-five years ago. Susie here was still in kindergarten when I had that job but you would have been at primary school.'

'Ah…'

The sound from Hugh was strangled. The sudden flick of a glance in Molly's direction gave her the impression that Hugh was taken aback enough to be having difficulty deciding how to react. He looked as if he was merely going to acknowledge the information and escape but Louise kept talking.

'We only worked together until your poor sister got so sick, of course. We all understood why she had to give it up and go on a benefit to look after her.' She was making that tutting sound again. 'Such a tragedy…she never got over it, did she? Your mum? And it was so hard on you when you were just a little boy yourself…'

Molly was watching Hugh's face as Louise prattled on but when she saw his head beginning to turn as if he wanted to know if she *was* watching him, she hurriedly looked away.

'Let me help you get Benji's clothes back on, Susan,' she said, a little more loudly and firmly than she would usually. 'Or maybe your mum would like to help.'

She was hoping that Susan's mother would take the hint and stop talking. Because Molly had seen the horror washing over Hugh's face and the rigid body language that was like a forcefield being erected and it was patently obvious that this was a subject that was not only private, but it was capable of causing anguish.

Molly could actually feel that pain herself, her heart was squeezing so hard. Something else was gaining strength rapidly as well—the urge to try and protect Hugh Ashcroft.

'Louise?' This time her tone was a command. 'Could you help us with Benji, please?'

'Oh…yes, of course…' Louise looked towards Molly, then swung her head back to the door but Hugh had vanished. Louise shrugged. 'It *was* a long time ago,' she muttered. 'Maybe he doesn't want to talk about it.'

Molly's smile was tight enough to advertise that she didn't want to talk about it, either, but Louise didn't seem to notice.

'Dear wee thing, his sister, Michelle. So pretty, with her golden hair that hung in real ringlets. Until it all fell out from the chemo, of course,' she added sadly.

Molly's response was a request. 'Could you get the hoodie jacket with the zip that matches these dinosaur pants, please, Louise? That will keep Benji nice and warm and it'll be easy to get on and off.'

Benji started crying as his mobile arm got lost inside the larger size tee shirt that had been purchased to fit over the cast.

'Got cancer, she did,' Louise continued as she went to the pile of clothing in the cot. 'When she was only about three, poor kid. Can't remember what sort it was but she was in and out of hospital for years and years and then she died. Never really saw Claire after that.'

She handed the jacket top to Molly, who was showing Susan how to position her hands to lift her top-heavy baby, who was now crying loudly. Susan looked as if she might start crying herself.

'She died not that long after. There were rumours that she'd taken some kind of overdose but I reckon it was down to her heart being broken so badly.' Louise must have realised that nobody was listening and gave up. 'Rightio…let Nana help you get your jacket on, Benji. We need to get you back home, don't we?'

Molly helped with getting the baby dressed and then left the women to pack the rest of their belongings to be ready for Benji's father, who was coming to collect them.

It wasn't that she hadn't been listening to Louise. Molly was professional enough to hate gossip but she couldn't deny that she had been listening avidly to every word. It explained so much, didn't it?

That aloofness.

The way he could be a completely different person when he thought he was totally alone and doing something, like surfing, that provided such an effective escape from the real world.

She could forgive the control he kept over himself. She could understand the distance he preferred to keep from others. How could he not have learned to protect himself from getting too involved?

Molly was still thinking about what she'd heard as she went to the next patient needing her attention. Thinking about the little boy that Hugh Ashcroft had been. A child who'd had to live with a terrible tragedy? It was the kind of story that would touch anyone's heart, but Molly Holmes had always been a particularly soft touch for a sad story.

And this one had already captured her heart completely.

Hugh stayed well away from the ward for the next few hours. Until he could be completely sure that Benji's grandmother would be nowhere on the grounds of Christchurch Children's Hospital.

It helped that, after a morning of scheduled surgeries, Hugh had a fully booked outpatient clinic for the afternoon. There was no time at all to dwell on the unpleasant pull into the past that Hugh had experienced in his visit to Benji's room and plenty of cases that were complex enough to need his full focus. Concentration that worked a treat until the last patient to be ushered into the consulting room for today's clinic.

Fourteen-year-old Michael had been a patient under Hugh's care for some years now.

'You've had a bit of a growth spurt, haven't you, Mike?'

'Just over eight centimetres,' his father said proudly. 'He's going to end up taller than me at this rate.'

'It's making his scoliosis worse, though, isn't it?' Michael's mother looked pale and worried. 'Is that why he's getting so short of breath lately?'

'It is,' Hugh agreed. 'Lung function is compromised because the diaphragm and chest wall muscles can't move the way they should. Is getting short of breath interfering with what you want to do, Michael?'

The teenager nodded. 'I can't go to the gym… I can't hang out with my mates at the skate park… It's hard to even walk…'

Listening to him speak made it very clear how far his lung function had deteriorated since Hugh had last seen him.

'His brace is hurting him, too,' his mother added.

'I'm not surprised,' Hugh murmured. He clicked his keyboard to bring up scan images taken only days ago. The screen showed a spinal column distorted enough to resemble a letter S.

'See that?' Hugh talked directly to Michael. 'You've now got a sixty-five-degree curve on the top of your spine and nearly eighty degrees on the bottom. Surgery is recommended when the scoliosis is over fifty degrees and, with the effect it's having on your breathing, I think it's becoming urgent.'

Michael's nod was solemn. 'You said this might happen one day—that I'd need an operation. I'm ready for it. You have to put rods and screws in my back, don't you?'

'And maybe some bone grafts. It's called a spinal fusion and it will straighten your back enough to make it easy to breathe again. I think you'll find you can do a lot more at the gym—and on your skateboard—but you'll have to be patient while you recover properly, okay?'

'Sure…' Michael's eye contact was brief and his tone just a little off-key. 'How soon can I get it done?'

He was scared, Hugh realised, but he didn't want anyone to know—his friends, his family or even his surgeon. He was young enough to crave comfort but old enough to know that adults had to be able to look after themselves. Maybe he didn't want his mother to be any more upset than she already was.

For a moment that was even briefer than that eye contact, Hugh remembered what it had been like when he was fourteen.

Being that scared even though it was for different reasons.

And being unbearably lonely at the same time.

Dammit…

This was because of Benji's grandmother. She'd known enough to invade his privacy and make it public that his younger sister had died from her cancer. That it had broken his mother irreparably. How much more did she know? And would she think it was so long ago it didn't matter if she shared it with others?

Like Molly Holmes…?

Hugh had the horrible feeling that Molly had seen more than he would want anybody to see but he'd been ambushed, hadn't he? He hadn't even known that he might need to be ready to protect himself from what had felt like a potentially lethal attack.

Hugh squashed the thought ruthlessly. This wasn't about him.

It was never about him. Not at work or away from it.

'Let's have a look at my schedule,' he said to Michael. 'It's a four-to-six-hour operation but you'll only need a few days in hospital. It'll be a bit longer before you can go back to school, though. When do the summer holidays start?'

'First week of December. But my exams will all be over in November.'

'Sounds like a plan,' Hugh said. 'It would be nice if you were back home and well into your recovery by Christmas, wouldn't it?'

Michael's mother was reaching for her husband's hand. 'That would be the best Christmas present we could get.'

It was nearly five o'clock by the time Hugh put his last folder of patient notes on the desk for the clinic administration staff to sort out.

Benji would have been discharged hours ago.

Molly would have finished her morning shift about the same time so there was no danger of being reminded of what he'd spent the whole afternoon trying to forget. It should be quite safe to go and check on his post-op patients from this morning. He needed to see the teenager who'd torn his anterior cruciate ligament playing a game of rugby and received a hamstring tendon autograft to repair it. He was a day-surgery patient and his registrars would have been monitoring him since he came out of Theatre but Hugh preferred to see all his patients himself before they were discharged.

'Have you had a chat to the physio?' he asked him. 'Did they check your brace and size the crutches for you?'

'They made me go up and down the stairs to make sure I know how to use them.'

'Good. And you've got an orthopaedic outpatient appointment set up?'

'Yes.'

'Excellent. You can go home.'

Hugh could go home, as well. He might even have time to get out to the beach and catch a wave or two before it got dark. Not at the beach where Molly lived, mind you. He wasn't planning to go back there any time soon.

Maybe it was because he was thinking about her that Hugh turned his head as he walked past the courtyard garden. She wasn't out there, of course, but it was all too easy to conjure up the memory of her dancing with her dog.

All too easy to feel a frisson of what he'd felt when he'd been watching her.

No. He certainly wasn't going to go back to that beach to surf again. He didn't want to meet Molly out of work hours again.

He wasn't too sure he wanted to meet her *during* work hours, in fact, so it was an unpleasant surprise to turn back from that glance into the garden to find her walking straight towards him.

As if he'd conjured *her* up along with that memory.

After this morning, he had more to worry about than a fleeting moment of attraction. She knew something about him that was personal. Something he didn't want to become common knowledge.

Hugh could feel his eyes narrowing. Because attack was the best form of defence, perhaps? 'What are you still doing here?' he demanded. 'I thought your shift finished a long time ago.'

'I stayed a bit longer,' Molly said. 'I was talking to Joanne Jacobs. Sophie's mother?'

'I know who she is.' Hugh was still watching her carefully but he couldn't see any sign that this was anything but a professional exchange. There was nothing to suggest she was interested in—or possibly had taken note of—anything personal about him at all.

'I'm just heading back to see her again. It was a pretty intense conversation. They're still struggling with the idea of the rotationplasty.'

Hugh's frown deepened. 'So I heard.'

'Well… I thought of something that might help—especially when they're talking to Sophie about it. I worked with a girl who had the procedure in Australia and she was a very keen dancer as well.'

'Oh...?'

It was there again, unbidden, in his head. A private video clip of Molly with her arms in the air, making a circle and then gracefully bending her body to bring the circle low enough for the dog to jump through.

'So... I went to print something out but then I wondered whether I should be getting this involved.' Molly was fishing in the pocket of her scrub tunic. 'Can I show you? I don't want to overstep boundaries or anything and she is your patient.'

Hugh blinked. Surely Molly had overheard what Benji's grandmother had said this morning? Was she just going to pretend it had never happened? That she wasn't aware of any personal information that was going to change their professional relationship?

Well...that was fine by him...

'What is it?' He had to admit he was curious.

Molly had rolled the sheet of photocopy paper so it didn't get creased. She unrolled it and Hugh's eyes widened.

It was an astonishing picture. A small girl—maybe eleven or twelve years old—was doing one of those ballet leaps that could make them look as if they were suspended in mid-air, with their arms and legs stretched out wide, if the photo was taken at precisely the right moment. The girl in this photo was looking straight at the camera as she jumped and she had a smile as wide as the reach of her arms, but what was truly remarkable was that one of her legs was a prosthesis.

Hugh could see in an instant, by the scarring high on her leg, that the girl had undergone the procedure of using the ankle as a new knee joint. The back-to-front foot was hidden inside the structure of the artificial leg and...there was a pale pink ballet shoe on the foot to match the one on the girl's normal leg.

'Her name's Amber,' Molly said. 'I don't feel like I'm invading her privacy because she—and her family—were so proud of this photo. Amber's the poster girl for the orthopaedic and prosthetic departments and this picture's on the website for the hospital I worked at in Australia.'

'So Sophie's family could find it themselves with an Internet search?'

'Yes...but Sophie's only seven and I thought she might like a real picture so that she could look at it whenever she wanted to.'

Hugh was having another one of those strange moments, like he'd had with Michael, when he'd been whisked back into the past to remember what it was like being a teenager. Now he was going even further back. To when his sister was so sick and she'd lost all her hair. She'd loved her ballet class, too, when she'd been well enough to attend. Would she have felt better if she'd seen a picture of a girl with no hair, doing a leap in the air like this, with the happiest smile in the world on her face?

His throat felt oddly tight. How good would *he* have felt as a big brother if he'd shown her that imaginary photograph and told her that it could be *her* doing that in the future? Michelle would have probably slept with the picture under her pillow and put it on the wall when she was in hospital, as she did with the one of Fudge—the family's chocolate brown Labrador.

Would Molly feel that good if it helped Sophie?

Hugh suspected she'd probably have to wipe a tear off her face—as he'd seen her do in that radiology room when Sophie had had her biopsy—except it might be a much happier tear this time.

He swallowed past the sudden lump in his own throat.

'I don't think you're overstepping any boundaries,' he said. 'Show it to Joanne first or perhaps the psychologist who's working with them.'

'Okay…thanks, Hugh.' Molly was rolling the paper up again.

'No…thank *you*…' he responded.

She caught his gaze, her eyes wide. 'What for?'

What for, indeed?

For going above and beyond any part of her job description—working overtime after an already long day without any financial reward for her efforts—to help the patients she was caring for on a very personal level?

For being the kind of person who would spend their days off doing the same thing by being a handler for a pet therapy programme?

Or was it deeper than that for Hugh? Was he thanking her for respecting his privacy? For making it clear she wasn't about to display curiosity, let alone try to get more information about his past?

Maybe it went even deeper than *that*.

Perhaps what Hugh was really thanking Molly for was making him feel that she was someone who could be trusted on a personal level, because people like that were few and far between in his life.

Pretty much non-existent, in fact.

And that made Molly Holmes rather special.

Not that he was about to tell her any of that. What he did do, however, was smile at her. A smile that felt like it was coming from somewhere he hadn't been in…what felt like for ever.

From right inside his heart?

'For doing something that might make a real difference,' was all he said. 'Good job, Molly.'

CHAPTER FIVE

THE OUTPATIENT CLINIC had finished long ago.

Almost all the department's ancillary staff members—the receptionists, technicians and nurses—had already left for the day. Hugh's registrars were up on the ward doing a final ward round and sorting any clinical issues.

Julie, the charge nurse manager, poked her head around the door of the consulting room Hugh had stayed in to snatch a few extra minutes of peace and quiet.

'Haven't you got a home to go to, Hugh?'

'I've got my last case notes to update. On Benji?'

'Oh, yes…isn't he doing well? He's crawling properly now instead of scooting along on his bottom to avoid putting any weight on the other shoulder.'

'Definitely a success story.'

'I didn't envy his mum having to look after him in that cast for so long, though I guess it's not as bad as a spica cast for hip dysplasia.'

'That's certainly harder to keep clean.' But Hugh turned back to the computer on his desk to indicate that he wanted to get on with making notes about how well Benji's clavicle had healed, not discuss how well his family had coped with the recovery period.

Julie took the hint and left but Hugh was aware of a remnant of thought about that patient interview that had nothing to do with anything clinical. Thankfully, Benji's grandmother hadn't come to this last appointment with her daughter but that hadn't stopped Hugh from remembering that encounter the day the toddler had been discharged after his operation.

And, as usual, that made him think about Molly Holmes.

He saw her all the time when she was working in his ward, mind you. He'd seen her quite often in the hospital on her days off when she brought her dog in for pet therapy sessions. He'd even seen her in the theatre suite once when she'd been with a child who was having a general anaesthetic induced and he had no problem with that. Hugh was more than happy that they were both far more comfortable around each other now than they had been when they'd first met but…

…but it was always just a bit disturbing when she entered his mind when she was not physically present in his environment.

When something reminded him that she had tapped into a space that nobody was allowed to enter by making him believe he could trust her. If anything, that feeling had grown a lot stronger because, in all the intervening weeks, Molly had never said or done anything to suggest that she intended to cross boundaries. She hadn't even given him one of those 'knowing' looks that women seemed to be so good at delivering.

It was getting less disturbing, however. Possibly because it happened so often? It was only yesterday when he'd gone to the paediatric oncology ward to see how Sophie Jacobs' latest round of neoadjuvant chemotherapy was going that he'd had a double whammy of being reminded, in fact. Sophie had that piece of A4 paper stuck onto the wall above her bed. The one Molly had printed out with the ballet dancer doing the leap with her prosthesis.

That reminded Hugh not only of that conversation they'd had about the image of someone dancing but of Molly herself dancing, with that dog. But that was exactly what Hugh needed to think of to flick the 'off' switch. Preferably before he was reminded of an attraction he had managed to gain complete control of.

He channelled that control into his fingers as he typed into the digital patient records.

The surgical intervention of the resection

and excision of the clavicular pseudoarthrosis, in conjunction with bone grafting using autograft tissue from the iliac crest and then internal fixation, has resulted in a very satisfactory bone union. The cosmetic result is pleasing and the patient is rapidly gaining full function of his shoulder joint.

That summed up the consultation well, along with the radiologist's comments on the latest X-rays and notes from the physiotherapist. There was only one thing to add.

There are no indications that further follow up is needed at this point although a second surgery in the future to remove the plates may be an option if implant prominence or irritation occurs.

Hugh saved his notes, logged out of the access to medical records and closed down the desktop computer.

Closing the door of the consulting room behind him, Hugh was startled by a clattering noise coming from the reception area. Surely he hadn't taken so long it was time for the cleaners to come through the deserted department?

And then he heard something so unexpected he couldn't quite place it.

Someone coughing?

A *dog's* bark?

And, dammit…there was Molly Holmes in his head again.

He walked past the reception desk and into the waiting area and somehow he wasn't even surprised to see that she was here in a physical sense as well.

With her dog.

No…make that *two* dogs…

Milo wasn't too sure about this.

He barked again and then crouched to deliver a growl that sounded way more playful than ferocious.

Was there really something scary about the spokes on the wheelchair parked in the corner of the waiting room? Or maybe it was being in the hospital environment with all its strange smells and noises and too many people and things on wheels.

'It's okay, Milo.' Molly reached into the pouch that was attached to a belt around her waist and took out a tiny treat to give to the young dog. 'I know it looks scary but it's just a wheelchair. Look—Oreo's not bothered at all, is she?'

But when she looked up, Oreo had uncharacteristically deserted her post where she was sitting at the end of a row of chairs and was heading straight for the person emerging from the back of the department. Fortunately, Oreo didn't bounce at Hugh Ashcroft. She just stopped in front of him and waved her tail in a polite greeting. His expression, however, was reminiscent of when he'd walked into Sophie Jacobs' bone biopsy appointment and had seen her there with Oreo.

Was this going to undo the growing ease that seemed to have developed between herself and Hugh in the last weeks? An edging closer that could possibly develop into a real friendship?

Sometimes, recently, when Hugh had smiled at her in passing, and even more when he'd caught her gaze deliberately, Molly had had moments of dreaming that something more than friendship could evolve. The way he was looking at her right now, however, suggested that any thoughts in that direction were purely one-sided.

'I'm so sorry.' Molly grimaced. 'My friend Julie told me it would be fine to bring Milo in for some training when the department was empty and before the cleaners came in. I thought today's clinics finished more than an hour ago.'

'They did. I stayed late.' Hugh stepped around Oreo without acknowledging the greeting he was being given. 'You have *two* dogs?'

'This is Milo. He's my mother's dog but I'm going to adopt him, at least for a while. Her retriever, Bella, has just had another litter of pups and it'll be too much for Milo when they get mobile. She kept him from the last litter because she thought he could be a good candidate as a therapy dog and I think she's right. He just needs to get some more exposure to clinical spaces and I knew that Orthopaedic Outpatients would have plenty of wheelchairs and walkers and crutches to make things interesting.'

While she was talking, Milo had bravely taken a step towards the wheelchair and stretched his nose out to sniff the unfamiliar object. Then he cringed and jumped backwards. Molly bit her lip. And then she glanced at Hugh.

'Have you got another minute or two to spare?'

'Why?'

'I think the wheelchair might be less threatening if it had someone sitting in it.'

'You want *me* to sit in the wheelchair?'

'You're a stranger. It would make it more realistic. I can go out and come in again and if you encouraged Milo, he might come and say hullo and realise the chair isn't going to bite him. He's very friendly and it'll only take a minute.' She gave Hugh her best smile. *'Please...?'*

She saw the hesitation but she shamelessly held his gaze because instinct told her that this was an opportunity to add something much more personal to their professional relationship and that was the only way this could turn into any kind of a real friendship.

Hugh shrugged. 'Why not? I owe you a favour.'

'Why?'

'Sophie Jacobs' parents signed the consent forms for the rotationplasty today. She's going to have the moulds of her foot made in the next few days and we can schedule her surgery after she's recovered from this round of chemo.'

'Oh…' Molly forgot about Milo's training for the moment, catching her bottom lip between her teeth again. 'That's *such* good news. And she'll be back in the orthopaedic ward for a while. I'll have to bring Oreo in to visit again.'

'It is good news. Having a visit from a lad who had the procedure a few years ago helped the decision making but it was that picture of yours that started the ball rolling in the right direction. Did you know that Sophie said "I want to be just like her" as soon as she saw it?'

Molly nodded. 'I was there. I knew that Joanne and Simon wanted to get her through the initial chemo before making a final decision, but I had a feeling they just needed the time to get used to what Sophie's leg was going to look like.'

Hugh was walking towards the wheelchair. Molly patted her leg and Milo obediently followed her into the side corridor without pulling on his lead. Oreo's gaze was on Hugh.

'Oreo, *down*,' Molly commanded. *'Stay.'*

With an audible thump, Oreo dropped to the floor and put her nose on her paws. Hugh sat in the wheelchair. When Molly walked back in she casually approached Hugh and he clicked his fingers at Milo.

'Hullo,' he said. 'Who's a good boy?'

Milo went straight towards him, his whole body wiggling with happiness at being noticed. Molly reached for a treat but Milo didn't notice because he was poking his nose around the wheel, trying to reach Hugh's hand for a pat.

She expected Hugh to pull back but, to her amazement, he was smiling at Milo, who nudged his hand so that it was automatic to fondle the dog's head and ears and then his neck.

'It's not so scary, is it?' Hugh looked up at Molly. 'Want me to roll around?'

'If you've got time, that would be fabulous.'

Milo leapt back as the wheelchair moved and Molly just let him watch. Oreo got up as the wheelchair went past her and started walking beside Hugh but Molly didn't tell her to stay again. It felt like she was showing Milo how it was done and, when Molly gave Milo some more length on the long lead, the young dog went straight towards them and walked behind Oreo.

They both got treats a few minutes later.

'Thank you so much,' Molly said to Hugh. 'I couldn't have done that by myself.' She smiled at him. 'I won't make you hop around on crutches or use a walker.'

Hugh made a huffing sound that was almost

laughter. 'I think I'd prefer to put off giving a walker a trial run.' He got up out of the wheelchair. 'I do happen to know when orthopaedic gear like this goes when it's out of date or deemed not worth repairing. Would it be helpful if you had some rusty crutches or an ancient wheelchair at home for training purposes?'

Molly nodded enthusiastically. 'That would be awesome. Let me know if there's anything available and I can pick it up. I've got a van.'

Oreo was following Hugh towards the doors that led from the outpatient department into the main corridor that joined the front foyer of the hospital.

'She really likes you,' Molly said. 'Sorry... I realise it's probably a one-sided attraction.'

Oh, *help*...had she really said that aloud? It sounded as if she was talking about herself and Hugh.

But Hugh didn't seem horrified. 'I don't dislike dogs,' he said. 'I grew up with one.' He paused and gave Oreo a pat. 'Fudge, his name was. He was a rather overweight chocolate Labrador. He lived to be fourteen, which was the same age I was at the time he died.'

'*Oh*...' Molly could feel her face scrunching into lines of sympathy. 'It must have been devastating to lose him. He'd been there for your whole life.'

Hugh was staring at her and Molly's heart sank. She'd crossed a line, here, hadn't she? Pushed herself into a personal space where she was definitely not welcome? Maybe this wasn't as bad as asking about his sister who'd died but it was pretty close. His dog would have been a huge part of his life. As important as another sibling, even...?

But Hugh's gaze dropped to Oreo again.

So did Molly's. She watched the gentle touch of his fingers as they traced Oreo's head and ear.

She could actually *feel* that touch herself and it was doing strange things to her body. No wonder Oreo's eyes were drifting shut in an expression of ecstasy.

'It was devastating enough to make me know I never wanted to do it again,' Hugh added quietly.

Molly swallowed. 'It's unbearably hard to lose dogs,' she agreed.

Hugh's hand lifted abruptly as though he'd just realised what he was doing. A look from Molly was enough to get Oreo to move back to her side and she clipped a lead onto the harness that was part of her service dog coat.

'But, for me,' she added, 'it would be even harder to live without them.'

The sound Hugh made was no more than a grunt. He was heading towards the doors again.

'I'll let you know if there's any unwanted mobility aids available.'

'Thank you. And thanks for your help. You don't owe me any more favours.' Molly wasn't sure if he could hear her as the doors swung shut behind him. 'You never did...'

He didn't owe her any more favours.

She'd told him she had a van and could collect any large items like an unwanted wheelchair. Maybe if it hadn't been a lightweight, easy-to-fold kind of wheelchair that still left space in the back of an SUV for a battered, old walking frame and some elbow crutches that had seen better days, Hugh wouldn't be driving out to Molly's house.

Except that it was something he wanted to do enough to overcome any doubts about whether or not it was something he *should* be doing.

It was a warm, late spring evening and, while it was too late to rope his surfboard to the roof rack and try to catch a wave, there was always a pull towards the beach and the sea for Hugh. Even filling his lungs with the smell of the ocean could be enough to tap into the freedom of being in the water—or, better yet, skimming the face of a wave that took him to a place where nothing else mattered.

Where there was nothing but the joy of utter freedom.

If Molly was on an afternoon shift she wouldn't be at home but that wasn't a problem. He knew which house was hers, having had it pointed out to him from the beach, and he would just leave the items on her doorstep. It might be better if that was the case, in fact, because one of the doubts Hugh had entertained—the *main* doubt— was that Molly might think he was coming on to her by turning up out of the blue.

Had that disturbing recognition of attraction not been completely quashed?

Was he coming on to her?

No. Hugh turned up the steep road that wound over the hill to Taylors Mistake beach. Of course he wasn't. The last thing he wanted was a relationship that would interfere with his life and he was confident that Molly probably felt the same way. Even if she was single, Molly had quite enough going on in her own life and, anyway— she wouldn't have the slightest interest in a man that she'd considered so uptight he might as well have been wearing a straitjacket.

So that made it feel safe.

And…it would be nice to have a friend.

Someone he could trust.

It was oddly disappointing when his knock on the door of the little white cottage with the red roof and the big chimney went unanswered but Hugh simply shrugged and went to unload the back of his vehicle. He could have a quick walk on the beach before he went home and that would make the journey more than worthwhile.

As he propped the elbow crutches inside the walking frame, however, he heard Molly's voice.

'*Yes*… Good girl, Oreo. Go… Go, go, *go*…'

It was a happy shout. There might have been some hand clapping going on as well and there was definitely an excited dog bark.

Hugh told himself he wasn't being nosy. It would simply be polite to let Molly know that he'd delivered the mobility aids, so he walked around the side of the house, stopping as he came to a long back garden that morphed into the marram grass covered sand dunes between the row of houses and the beach.

There was some kind of obstacle course laid out on the coarse grass of a beachside lawn.

Molly was still shouting.

'*Jump*… Good girl… And over the seesaw… *yes*…'

The jump was a tree branch of driftwood set on top of two wooden crates. The seesaw was a long plank of wood balanced on an empty forty-gallon drum that must have come from a farm. So had that tractor tyre that was suspended above the ground to make a hoop that Oreo had been jumping through as Hugh stopped to watch. Neither dog nor handler noticed him. Oreo raced up the thin plank of wood on the drum, stopped for a moment to let the wood tilt down on the other side and then she was off again. Over the jump from another direction, through a bending tunnel that was the only part of the course that didn't look homemade and then she was weaving through a set of poles in the ground.

Molly was as focussed as Oreo and clearly loving it just as much. She ran beside her dog, making a hand signal to encourage a jump, clapping to emphasise something good—even running with her head down herself as Oreo went flat to run through the tunnel.

She was wearing ancient denim shorts that looked like cut-off jeans judging by their frayed hems, and a tee shirt that was knotted on one side to make it fit close to her body. Her hair was loose—a wild mop of black curls—her face was pink from exertion and she was out of breath when she held out her arms to Oreo to jump into for a hug.

She was laughing as she put Oreo down and straightened, which was the moment she saw Hugh standing there.

And…it made Hugh suddenly feel as happy as he felt when he was riding a particularly good wave. As if he were flying.

As if there was nothing he needed to worry about in this moment.

As if he was free…

'Oh, my goodness… *Hugh*…?'

Oreo went straight towards Hugh and sat in front of him.

'Sorry to interrupt,' he said. 'I brought some old mobility gear for you, like the wheelchair you wanted. They're by your front door.'

'Oh, wow…thank you *so* much. That's fantastic.' Molly was pushing curls damp with perspiration back from her face. That wild hair was framing a face that clearly didn't have a scrap of makeup on it and…

…and…she looked absolutely gorgeous.

Stunning, even…

Oreo barked at Hugh as if she were trying to cut his train of thought and he was grateful enough to smile at the dog and reach down to pat her head.

'She wants to play,' Molly told him. 'She wants you to do her agility course with her.'

Hugh shook his head. 'I wouldn't know how.'

'She'll show you.' Molly was grinning at him. 'You'll love it, I promise. It's more fun than surfing.'

'Impossible.'

'You won't know until you try. Go on… I *dare* you…'

A tumble of thoughts raced through Hugh's mind. That Molly was encouraging him the way she had been urging Oreo on? That if he ever wanted a chance to prove he wasn't as uptight as Molly thought he was, this might be the best opportunity ever. That this was the kind of light-hearted stuff that friends could enjoy doing together and…

…and that smile was simply irresistible.

'Fine.' Hugh loosened his tie and pulled it off. He rolled up the sleeves of his shirt. 'Come on, Oreo.'

Molly called directions. 'Over the jump. Follow Oreo to the A frame… Now get ahead of her, point to the jump and then head for the seesaw…'

It was only Hugh who needed the directions. Oreo knew the course by heart and was so happy to be showing off to Hugh that she kept barking, even as she disappeared into the tunnel and then weaved at incredible speed back and forth through the poles.

Hugh was laughing himself by the time he got back to Molly, despite being completely out of breath.

'Hold out your arms,' Molly commanded. 'It's not finished until Oreo gets her cuddle.'

Without thinking, Hugh held out his arms and suddenly they were full of the warmth and hairiness of a large dog. He was getting licked on his neck and…this was another kind of happy, wasn't it? He hadn't been this close to a dog since he'd hugged Fudge before he went to school.

The day he'd come home to find he wasn't lying there at the gate with his ball safely between his paws, waiting for their game. And he never would be again…

Hugh crouched to let Oreo slip from his arms to the ground. Molly's smile was still doing something unusual to his brain. For the first time ever, he was thinking of Fudge and remembering the joy of being with him was overriding the sadness of losing him.

'Well…that *was* fun,' he admitted. 'But it doesn't beat surfing.'

'I can't believe you actually did that.' Molly was biting her lip as if she was trying not to grin too widely. 'I was so wrong about you…'

Her smile had faded and her gaze was fixed on his. He could see the way her bottom lip almost bounced free of her teeth and the appreciation in Molly's eyes made him want to turn back and do that obstacle course with Oreo all over again.

No…

What it *really* made him want to do was to kiss Molly.

For a long, long moment, Hugh couldn't breathe. It felt like he didn't need to because time had stopped. He couldn't look away from those golden-brown eyes, either. It was probably only for a heartbeat—maybe two, but it was long enough for something to force its way into his head.

A cloud that was dark enough to obliterate any sunshine.

Fear...?

He jerked his gaze away from Molly's. He pretended to look at his watch.

'Is that the time?' What a stupid thing to say. 'I have to go,' he added. 'I've got a lot of prep to start getting done tonight.'

'Oh...?'

Molly sounded slightly bewildered. When he sneaked a lightning-fast glance as he turned away, she wasn't looking at him.

'Yes. It's Sophie's surgery the day after tomorrow. We've got a full team meeting to plan the surgery in detail tomorrow and I want to be well prepared for that.'

'It must be a big deal. You're basically reattaching an amputation, aren't you?'

'Yes.' This was better. Professional conversation. And Hugh was on his way to escape.

'Do you have vascular surgeons involved? And neuro?' Molly asked.

'It's a huge team. And there's a lot of interest with it being an unusual procedure, so it's in the main theatre with the gallery.'

Hugh was feeling almost safe again as he got closer to his car. He was also feeling a bit embarrassed. How rude did Molly think he was, running off like this?

'Why don't you come and watch as well, if you're not working?' he suggested. 'It's a long surgery but not something you get to see every day.'

Molly's intake of breath was an excited gasp. '*Could* I? It *is* a day off for me.'

'You're part of the extended team involved in Sophie's care and I know that this surgery might not be happening if it hadn't been for you. I can make sure there's a front row seat saved for you.'

There…the movement of time and tide were completely back to normal.

If Molly had been aware of any inappropriate and/or unwanted notions that had entered Hugh's head when he'd been staring at her like some lust-struck teenager, she had forgotten all about it now.

She was biting her lip again and her eyes were shining. 'I can't wait.'

CHAPTER SIX

HE'D ALMOST KISSED HER.

Hugh Ashcroft had actually been thinking about *kissing* her.

Oh, *my*…

As she slipped into the seat on one end of the front row in the gallery above Theatre One, the only thing Molly would have expected to be thinking about was how exciting it was going to be watching some extraordinarily rare orthopaedic surgery.

'Scalpel, please.'

Hearing Hugh's voice through the speakers on either side of the enclosed gallery area should have been enough to focus absolutely on what she could see on the screens beside the speakers, which gave a close up, 'surgeon's eye' view of what was happening below them. Having an audience was clearly no distraction for Mr Ashcroft but, even through the glass, perhaps he was aware that everyone was holding their breath, waiting for the first incision. He had to know they would appreciate every bit of detail he was able to share.

'So our first incision is longitudinal below the groin and this gives us access for the dissection of the femoral artery and vein.'

Yeah…the ultimately professional, *impersonal* tone of his voice should have made Molly sit forward and focus on what she had come to see. But what she was, in fact, thinking about as that first incision was made was that the gowned and gloved surgeon standing beside the small, draped shape on the operating table had been so close to kissing her the day before yesterday that she could still feel her toes curling.

'I'm clamping the femoral artery to prevent bleeding during the surgery and now we'll extend the incision.'

Molly needed to clamp the direction her thoughts were going in. She focussed on the screen as vessels and nerves were slowly and painstakingly revealed and the specialist microvascular surgeon working with Hugh took over, giving a commentary on everything she was doing, such as the continuous dissection of the sciatic nerve behind the leg muscle. These important structures would be kept separated and completely intact while the middle section of the leg was removed.

This was a surgery that would take from six

to eight hours and there were long periods of intense and often silent work going on.

And Molly couldn't stop her gaze drifting from the close-up screen back to where Hugh had his head bent, looking into the actual operating field. He was completely covered with sterile fabric and a hat and mask and eyewear but, with his head bent like that, Molly could see a patch of skin at the back of his neck and she could feel a sensation deep in her belly as if something was melting.

She couldn't stop her thoughts drifting back to what could have ended up being a kiss.

Had she *wanted* Hugh to kiss her?

Judging by the sharp spear of sensation that obliterated the melting one, the answer to that question was resoundingly affirmative. The sexual attraction was real.

In retrospect, Molly was surprisingly disappointed that Hugh *hadn't* kissed her.

How ridiculous was that?

Even if she was ready to start looking for someone to fill the life partner-shaped gap in her life, Hugh Ashcroft would not be a contender.

Why not?

Molly ignored the little voice at the back of her mind and tuned back into what was happening on the screen. More incisions were being made and the surgical teams were discussing where to cut the bones of the upper and lower legs to leave sufficient margins to healthy tissue.

Minutes ticked on and turned into hours. People around Molly in the tiered seating, mostly wearing surgical scrubs themselves, came and went as they got paged or finished their breaks or needed to grab something to eat but Molly didn't move from her privileged spot in the front row. And, as fascinated as she was, her focus definitely faded at times.

Enough for that little voice to make another attempt.

Why not? You mean you don't believe that the right man might be just around the next corner in your life, like you keep telling yourself? Does Hugh not even make a shortlist?

No, Molly told herself.

Give me one good reason.

I can give you more than one. The first is that we work together and you know as well as I do that my last relationship was with Jonathon who I also worked with and that was the most spectacular disaster in my entire history of relationships that haven't worked out. I walked away from my job as well as that relationship. It felt like my life was completely broken.

Maybe that was because he didn't want Oreo as part of his life and that was just a cover for not wanting kids and then it turns out that he never

*wanted an exclusive relationship. You were just
part of a harem...*

Thanks for the reminder.

Molly shut the conversation down.

She didn't need reminding that she'd come
home to her family and a place she loved in order
to try and repair her life once and for all.

She didn't need reminding that her heart was
too easy to capture.

Too easy to break.

Molly was actually scared of that happening
again. What if it was the last straw and she could
never put the pieces back together again?

That fear should be more than enough to silence any notion that she might want to be kissed
by Hugh Ashcroft.

Besides, it was getting to the most fascinating
part of this operation anyway.

'So...those are the wires in place to mark
where the incisions will be made. They'll allow
me to pass a suture around the exact level I want
to cut the bone and we'll clamp that to the Gigli
saw.' Hugh turned to his scrub nurse. 'I'll have
a tonsil clamp, thanks, and then I'll be ready for
the braided suture.'

Molly found she was holding her breath as
she watched the absolute focus Hugh had on his
task—so much so, she could sense it in every
muscle of his body. She could watch his hands

close up on the screen and was riveted by the precision and care he was taking to do everything perfectly and make clean cuts through both the femur and the tibia, protecting the surrounding tissue as much as possible.

And then came the most astonishing moment of this surgery as the middle section of the small leg, which contained the tumour, was lifted clear and then sent to the laboratory for examination. In the space on the table, the arteries, veins and nerves that had been so painstakingly detached from the section that contained the tumour still joined the top of the leg to the ankle and foot.

'Now comes the part that will determine the success of this surgery.' Hugh's serious tone of voice came quietly through the speakers. 'We'll rotate the foot and ankle one hundred and eighty degrees in the axial plane and then join the femur and tibia with a dynamic compression plate. I'll hand over to my microsurgery colleagues at that point to re-join the blood vessels and nerves.'

The microsurgery was fascinating to watch and Molly had no intention of leaving until everything was finished, but she found herself sneaking glances to where Hugh was assisting rather than leading this part of the surgery instead of watching only the screen where so many tiny stitches were being placed to join structures that were so small it was hard to see exactly what was happening.

It was no surprise that her attention span was getting harder to maintain. That her thoughts, along with her gaze, drifted back to Hugh yet again.

Reason number two for Hugh to not make any shortlist for a potential life partner popped into her head with startling clarity. It wasn't simply that they were colleagues that made him similar to her last spectacular error of judgement.

He didn't like dogs any more than Jonathon did.

Oh, yeah? You didn't think so when he and Oreo were having the time of their lives running around the agility course.

Molly couldn't argue with herself over that point.

Both dog and man had clearly been enjoying themselves and that had shown her another glimpse of a very different Hugh Ashcroft. Like seeing him at one with the ocean when he was surfing had done.

She was beginning to think that she might be seeing the *real* Hugh through cracks in the persona that the majority of people in his life were permitted to see.

And what about Fudge? A dog he'd lost in a vulnerable part of his adolescence and it had hit him hard enough he was never going to go there again. He didn't even want to connect with someone *else's* dog. Had Oreo sensed that? Was that why she'd been so polite—gentle, even—in her approach to Hugh? Sitting there like a canine rock when he probably didn't notice the way he was stroking her ears as he talked about Fudge?

Well…both man and dog had let go of the barriers stopping them connecting when they'd done the agility course together, hadn't they?

Had that been the reason Hugh had done something as unexpected as almost kissing her?

Oh…

There it was again…

That delicious flicker of attraction. A flame that was resisting any attempts to douse it. The sensible part of her head hadn't stopped trying, however.

I don't even know if he's single, it announced. He could be married for all I know—not everybody wears a ring. Maybe he's even got a few kids.

But the part of herself she was arguing with didn't even bother to respond. They both knew how unlikely that was. With the kind of hours Hugh worked and his dedication, it seemed far more likely that he was married only to his job. Watching him at work like this had been impressive and Molly could be absolutely certain that he hadn't been distracted for a moment by her presence in the gallery or any memory of what had—almost—happened between them.

Her interest in this surgery hadn't been exaggerated, had it?

Hugh hadn't expected Molly to stay and watch the entire operation but he'd been aware of her presence from the moment he'd entered this theatre and had seen her sitting on the end of the front row.

The awareness was far enough in the background of his consciousness to have no bearing on his focus. It was just there, like a faint hum that added something extra to his normal determination to do the best possible job that could be done. This was someone who had cared enough about this patient to have gone to the trouble of finding that picture of the girl dancing with her rotationplasty prosthesis. To happily give the time and effort that bringing her dog in to dance for Sophie had required.

This mattered to Molly.

She was still there when Hugh was checking the perfusion of the reattached foot, feeling for a palpable pulse and noting the acceptable skin colour, but she had gone when Hugh glanced up to the gallery after the final closure of the wound.

He stayed to supervise the final dressing where

they would be using soft, orthopaedic wool as a thick bandage under the plaster cast to prevent too much pressure on repaired vessels and nerves as they healed. He was still there in the recovery room a while later as Sophie regained consciousness enough for him to be able to check for the first indication that nerve function was still intact. It was a very satisfying moment when the drowsy, heavily medicated little girl managed a tiny movement in her ankle joint when asked.

Hugh went to meet her anxious parents, able to tell them that the surgery had gone as well as they could have hoped for.

'She'll be taken up to the intensive care unit soon and will stay there for twenty-four to forty-eight hours.'

'Can we go and see her?'

'Of course. I'll get a nurse to take you in. The ICU consultant who'll be in charge of her care while she's in the unit is in with her now.'

'Thank you *so* much, Mr Ashcroft. You must be exhausted after being in Theatre for so long today.'

'It's what I do,' Hugh said simply. 'And when it goes this well, it's the best job in the world.'

He had to admit he *was* exhausted after so many intense hours of concentration—on his feet, and under the glare of artificial light—and Hugh knew he should really take a break after he'd done a brief ward round of his inpatients. He would have his phone by his side at all times and he'd come back in an hour or two to check on Sophie again, but she was stable enough to make any complications unlikely and there was a huge team of specialists in intensive care and paediatric oncology who had already taken over the primary care for this little girl in the post-operative phase of her treatment.

Going home to his inner-city apartment for a break wasn't attractive. Hugh needed some fresh air and whatever real daylight was left for the day. He could have headed into the centre of the city to the huge park and had a walk but, as he drove out of the hospital car park, he found himself following the line of hills on the southern city border. Heading for the place that would restore his energy levels and alertness faster than anywhere else.

He could have turned to his left a short time later to get to the beach that was closest to work but it seemed a no-brainer to turn right. To get to a beach that was far less likely to be crowded by other people shedding any stress from their working day. A beach that was his favourite but that he hadn't been back to since that surprise meeting with Molly after he'd gone surfing. And, after his visit to her little white cottage, he hadn't expected to ever come here again. Because he was sensible enough to heed an alarm when it sounded. Especially when he knew exactly *why* it was sounding.

Not that Hugh had consciously given it any thought since then, but he was well aware that if he hadn't grappled control back from the brink of losing it, he would have ended up kissing Molly Holmes completely senseless.

Because a tiny part of him suspected that she might have wanted him to?

Not that it mattered right now. Because control had been regained and he was far too drained after a marathon surgery to be remotely interested in thinking about something that would be disturbing.

Surfing would have been the best option but that wasn't possible when Hugh needed to be within earshot of his phone in case he had a call regarding Sophie's condition, but just a barefoot walk on the sand and some deep breaths of sea air should do the trick. It wouldn't take long.

Had Molly felt the same way after her long day in the gallery?

Was that why he could see the black and white shape of her dog running in the shallows as he stepped onto the beach?

But where was Molly?

Oreo was barking now and, instead of scanning the beach to look for a woman holding a frisbee, Hugh looked in the opposite direction. Thanks to following Oreo's line of sight, he could see past the break of the first wave and…good grief…was that Molly swimming? Without a wetsuit? At this time of the year the water would still be icy.

She was on her way back to shore but it wasn't until she reached the shallows and a relieved Oreo that Hugh realised how much less than a figure covering wetsuit Molly was wearing. She was in a rather scant bikini that showed off every curve of her body.

Every rather delicious curve…

She came out of the water at a run, heading straight for a crumpled towel on the sand and, even at this distance, Hugh could see how cold she looked.

Oreo was shaking water out of her coat as Molly snatched up the towel.

'Hey…' Hugh was close enough to call a greeting. 'That was brave. You must be absolutely freezing.'

'Hugh…' Molly stopped rubbing at her hair and held the towel in front of her. There were goosebumps on the skin of her arms and he saw her suppress a shiver. 'What on earth are you doing here?'

'I needed a break and some fresh air.'

'I'll bet… I was drained enough from just watching what you've been doing all day.' Molly was clutching the towel in front of her body now.

Hiding…?

But she was grinning. 'If you really want to wake yourself up, go and have a dip in those waves. It's gorgeous.'

'I haven't got anything to swim in.'

Her eyes widened in mock shock. 'Are you telling me you don't wear any undies, Mr Ashcroft?'

Nobody ever talked to him like this. Probably because he looked—and behaved—like someone who couldn't take a joke or a bit of teasing? Hugh's lips twitched. Maybe being unexpectedly teased like this was almost as good as fresh air and sunlight for getting rid of accumulated tension. But old habits died hard, as they said.

'I'm not about to put my underwear on public display,' he said.

Uh-oh…that was the kind of thing someone who was uptight enough to be repressed and prudish might say, wasn't it?

'I haven't got a towel,' he added, realising that sounded just as lame the moment he uttered the words.

But Molly was still grinning. 'I'll share mine,' she offered. 'Go on…you know you want to.'

And, astonishingly, Hugh knew she was right.

He *did* want to. He wanted to shake off the tension and stress of an extraordinarily intense day by doing something a bit crazy.

But he still shook his head. He could never be tempted enough to turn his back on the most important thing in his life. 'I can't leave my phone. I'm on call in case there are any complications with Sophie.'

'Are you expecting any?'

'No. She was looking great when I left Recovery. She could even move her ankle for me.'

'No *way*...' Molly's jaw dropped. 'That's amazing. I'm so happy to hear she's doing well. And hey... I can guard your phone and answer it if necessary. I can guarantee you won't need more than about sixty seconds in that surf to get the full recuperative benefits.'

The Hugh who'd never met Molly Holmes and her dogs would never have been so impulsive. He would have simply found another excuse not to do something as unconventional and potentially humiliating as running into the ocean in his underwear but...

...it appeared that Hugh wasn't quite the same man as he'd been a couple of months ago.

Because he handed his phone to Molly and stripped off his clothes. He didn't unbutton more than the second button of his shirt—he just yanked it over his head. Even Oreo seemed to be staring at him in disbelief but then she barked her approval and ran with him as he splashed through the shallow water until he could dive under a wave. And Molly was right, sixty seconds would have been more than enough to wash off every ounce of fatigue and pang of discomfort in overused muscles, but he stayed in twice as long, just to make sure.

If he'd stayed in any longer, he might have acclimatised to the chill water and been able to enjoy a swim, but Hugh was too conscious of needing to be near his phone so he came out of the water and got hit by the wind chill, even though it was only a mild sea breeze.

He reached for the towel Molly held out to him.

'No calls,' she told him. 'I was right, wasn't I? It was worth having a dip.'

'So worth it.' Hugh nodded.

'Better than surfing?' she suggested.

He shook his head. 'No...and I'll let you know later if it was really worth the hypothermia.'

Molly's towel was already damp so wasn't very effective in drying his skin, so Hugh was shivering uncontrollably before he'd rubbed more than half his body with the towel and Molly, who now had an oversized jumper on over her bikini, was biting her lip and looking—a little repentant?

Cute...

'You'd better come and stand under a hot shower for a minute,' she told him. 'Otherwise you'll never get properly warm again. Come on…' She didn't give him the chance to respond through his chattering teeth. Worse, she swooped on his pile of clothing and grabbed his shirt and trousers and then took off towards the sand dunes and the row of houses.

And she was still in possession of his phone!

Oreo looked torn for the space of two seconds and then took off after Molly.

There was nothing Hugh could do, other than pick up his shoes that had his socks stuffed inside them and go after them. By the time he went inside the cottage, Molly already had the shower running.

'Help yourself to shampoo or anything,' she invited. 'I'll get you a clean towel.'

The shower was over an old, clawfoot bath with just a curtain to stop the water splashing into the room. Hugh didn't peel off his sodden boxer shorts until he was safely behind the curtain, under the rain of water that felt hot enough to scald his chilled skin. He stayed under it for about as long as he'd been in the ocean and then reached to turn off the tap.

'Don't turn it off…' Molly was back in the bathroom. 'I need to jump in myself and the plumbing can be a bit temperamental. I'll put your towel by the basin, okay?'

'Thanks.' Hugh poked his head around the

edge of the curtain to see Molly about to drop the towel near where she'd left his phone beside a glass that held a toothbrush and tube of toothpaste.

Her toothbrush. Hugh could suddenly imagine Molly wearing nothing but a towel herself, standing in front of that mirror to clean her teeth last thing at night. And then two things hit him like a ton of bricks.

Molly was still wearing nothing but those two rather small scraps of fabric under that jumper.

And *he* was no more than a few inches away from her and was wearing absolutely nothing at all…

No…make that three things. Because now Hugh was thinking of the gorgeous curves of her body and the perfection of her smooth, olive skin being marred by goosebumps. In retrospect, he knew he'd been wondering what it would feel like to run his fingers, oh, so lightly over those goosebumps.

Would they reappear if he helped her peel that woollen jumper off?

Oh…*help*…

In the same instant a wave of that attraction that had almost made him kiss her—something he'd thought had been dealt with and banished—washed over him with even more of a shock than plunging into the icy sea so recently, Hugh noticed that Molly was watching *him*.

In the mirror.

It still felt like direct eye contact when he met her gaze, though.

Until she turned to face him and the touch of their gazes became suddenly searing. She still had the towel in her hand and, instead of dropping it, she held it out so that he could take it before he stepped out from behind the curtain. He knotted it loosely around his waist the moment his feet hit the floor.

Because he needed to hide the reaction his body was having to that wash of attraction that had somehow morphed into a level of desire like nothing Hugh had ever experienced in his life.

Molly couldn't move.

She couldn't breathe.

The universe seemed to be holding its breath as well as she simply stood there, holding that gaze for moment after moment after moment…

Until Hugh took one step closer, slid his fingers into her salt-tangled curls to hold her head and leaned down to cover her lips with his own.

Of course he knew it was what she wanted. A whole silent conversation had just been held in that prolonged eye contact. Questions asked…

Permission given…

No…maybe Molly had actually begged a little for this to happen…

The shower was still running behind him, which made it sound as if they were standing in a heavy rain shower, and the small room was filled with the warmth and steam of it. It was filled even more with the astonishing power of what was overwhelming every one of Molly's senses.

Hugh…

The taste of him.

The pressure of his lips.

The sliding dance of his tongue as he deepened a kiss that had already woken up every cell in Molly's body.

She felt his hands beneath the hem of her jumper now, sliding up her skin towards her breasts. Her hands followed his so that she could pull this unwanted piece of clothing off. To clear away a bulky obstacle, hopefully before he changed his mind and vanished again.

Hugh's lips and tongue were on the skin of her neck and shoulder moments later.

'You taste like the sea…'

Molly shivered. Partly because of the shaft of desire taking over her body but also because she was still wearing a damp bikini and her skin was sticky with sea salt. Chilled enough for it to be making Hugh's lips and tongue feel like flames licking her skin.

'You're cold…' Hugh's towel was falling to the floor as he took her hand. 'Come…'

He helped her step over the edge of the bath into the rain of the hot water. He helped her peel off her bikini top and bottom. And then he kissed her again.

A fierce kiss…

A need like none she had ever experienced took over Molly's body—and mind. There was danger here but there was no turning back. The sound Hugh made as she pressed herself even closer to his body could have been one of frustration—as if he was about to make this stop because he, too, had recognised it wasn't safe?

'No…'

It wasn't really a word. More like a sound of desperate need as Molly ran her hands down Hugh's back until she found the iron-hard muscle of his buttocks and shaped them with her hands. Pulled them closer.

The sound Hugh made then was more like a sigh of defeat. Or submission?

His hands were gripping Molly's bottom now. Lifting her so that she could wrap her legs around him. Holding her so they could find their balance and rhythm and give in to the waves of desire that were building to a climax like no other.

It was over too soon.

But not quite soon enough because the hot

water that Molly's cottage had available was running out and the shower was already cooling down fast.

At least that interrupted what could have been an awkward moment as Molly's feet touched the enamelled surface of the bath. Even eye contact was avoided for a few seconds as she climbed out and Hugh turned the tap off, she handed him his towel and reached for another one on a towel rail.

When they did finally make eye contact again, Molly raised her eyebrows. She wanted to lighten what was threatening to become an atmosphere they might both find too much, too soon.

'Better than surfing?' The words came out as a husky kind of whisper.

Hugh had to clear his throat before he could speak.

'Maybe...' he said.

His smile and tone suggested that it was possible he might need to experience it again to be sure.

And Molly smiled back. She wasn't about to object.

Maybe it could have happened then. In a comfortable bed. If the sound from Hugh's phone hadn't changed everything.

'It can't be anything urgent.' He picked up his phone. 'It's only a text message.' He looked up from the screen a moment later. 'Sophie's properly awake,' he told Molly. 'She's just moved the toes on her reattached foot.'

The very personal ground they had been on was being blurred into something professional and it felt…uncomfortable? Molly was quite certain that the last thing Hugh would want to talk about now was sex.

'I'll let you get dressed,' she said quietly. 'You'll want to go in and see her.'

She let her gaze graze his as she slipped out of the bathroom to find her own clothes. Less than a split second of contact but it was enough to let her know that Hugh appreciated that she understood.

His work always came first.

CHAPTER SEVEN

MAYBE SHE'D IMAGINED that unbelievable encounter in her bathroom.

She'd certainly *re*imagined it, more than once, during the somewhat sleepless night she'd just had.

But the version of Hugh Ashcroft that Molly encountered when she took Oreo into the children's hospital the next afternoon bore no resemblance at all to the man with whom she'd had the sexiest, most passionate encounter of her life less than twenty-four hours earlier.

He was back to being the version of the distant and disapproving surgeon she'd first encountered in that radiology procedure room.

Did he regret what had happened between them?

He certainly hadn't appeared to feel like that when he'd paused long enough to place a lingering kiss on her lips before he'd left the cottage.

Was he concerned that the information might be welcomed into the gossip mill with even more fascination than what Molly already knew about his private life?

No...surely Hugh knew that any trust in her was not misplaced?

Molly was the one who should be concerned. She'd allowed this gorgeous but complicated man to capture her heart and now she'd allowed him close enough to capture her body. They had to be the most significant building blocks to falling head over heels in love with someone and Molly wasn't at all sure she was at a point where she could halt that process if—or *when*—it became a matter of self-protection.

If she had her heart broken again this soon, she might never find the courage to let someone else this far into her life. Ever.

Perhaps that look was simply because Hugh felt it was a step too far, taking Oreo into the paediatric intensive care unit where Sophie Jacobs was in the early stages of her post-operative recovery? Oreo was on her very best behaviour, thank goodness, and she had waited for a signal that it was a time no other patients in the unit or their families might be disturbed. They had probably not even noticed her arrival because the rooms that opened onto the central space with the nurses' station and banks of monitoring equipment were very private, especially when the curtains were drawn across the internal windows.

The unit staff had also been consulted about this visit but…

…maybe Hugh was being reminded of the first time he'd seen a dogtor near one of his patients and maybe he was a bit shocked by how much had changed between himself and Molly since then…

Sophie was in a nest of soft pillows, her leg well supported and stable. Molly could just see an oxygen saturation probe clipped to the big toe of her reattached foot. She had electrodes on to monitor her heart and an automatic cuff to take her blood pressure. There were IV lines to deliver medications including the pain relief she was having and other tubes snaked from beneath a light, brightly coloured bed cover. With no hat on to cover her bald scalp, Sophie looked so incredibly vulnerable, it would be no surprise that some people might think it was totally inappropriate to have an animal in here who could potentially disrupt such a delicately balanced, technical set up.

But Sophie's mother was crying softly when she saw Molly and Oreo. 'I'm so glad you could come,' she said. 'Soph made me promise that she'd be able to see Oreo as soon as she woke up. I wasn't sure you'd be allowed in here but I said "yes" because that was what she wanted more than anything…'

'We can only stay for a few minutes.' Molly glanced over her shoulder, knowing that they were being carefully watched by staff members, including Hugh, who was talking to one of the intensive care consultants. 'This is the first time pet therapy has happened in the ICU here.'

She held Oreo's leash close to the clip on her harness and made sure the dog didn't get near any tubes or lines. She put a towel on the edge of Sophie's bed and tapped it to tell Oreo where to put her chin.

'Sophie?' Joanne was on the other side of the bed, stroking Sophie's head. 'Are you awake, darling? Guess who's come to see you…'

Eyelashes fluttered but Sophie was reaching out with her hand before she opened her eyes.

'*Aww…*' Her lips were curving into a smile. 'It's Oreo…'

The small hand had found Oreo's nose and fingers traced their way up to find her head and ears. Her dog might have been poked in the eyes on the way because Molly could see her blinking, but Oreo didn't move a muscle. She barely waved her tail and she didn't take her gaze off Sophie's face.

Molly had to fight back tears. She was *so* proud of Oreo.

She could see the emotion on Joanne's face as her daughter got the gift she'd wanted the most in this difficult time. Even Sophie's nurse, who was taking photos of this visit, was using a tissue to blot her eyes.

Molly didn't know whether Hugh had witnessed the joy. By the time Molly led Oreo quietly out of the unit a few minutes later, he could have been long gone. She didn't head straight back to her van in the car park, however. Because it had been such a short visit to the ICU, Molly thought she'd leave via her ward to see if there was another child who might like a visit from Oreo. And, when the doors of the lift slid open on the ward floor, she saw Hugh walking away from his office in the company of a very distressed looking woman.

Oreo picked up on the emotional intensity the moment she stepped out of the lift. She sat down, refusing to move any further towards the ward, and waited for Hugh to get closer.

He'd never been so relieved to be offered such an irresistible distraction.

Not only was his own mind diverted by a flash of how it had felt, albeit briefly, to be in a parallel universe with Molly Holmes yesterday evening, the distraught woman with him—Annabelle Finch—seemed to be having a reprieve from any aftermath of the awful conversation he'd just had with her.

She was veering towards Oreo.

'Oh…aren't you gorgeous?' Annabelle still had tears on her cheeks as she looked at Molly. 'Am I allowed to pat him?'

'Of course.' Molly smiled.

'She's a girl.' It was Hugh who made the correction. 'This is Oreo, Annabelle. She belongs to Molly, here, and she's trained to visit children as an assistance dog.'

He was also looking directly at Molly and had to ignore an odd squeeze in his chest as she shifted her gaze to catch his. This was definitely not the time to allow any pull towards what had happened between himself and Molly.

'This is Annabelle,' he said. 'She's Sam's mum. Sam is one of my patients.'

Annabelle was on her knees now, her cheek on Oreo's neck as she hugged the dog. 'Sam would love you,' she said. 'He's been begging me for a puppy for months now and…and I was planning to get one after the end of his chemo—in time for Christmas…' She turned to bury her face in Oreo's thick coat just in time to stifle a sob.

Hugh could feel his whole body tensing. Trying not to be pulled into this mother's pain. It was quite noticeably a much harder ask than normal. Because Molly was standing so close and his body was desperate to remind him of how it felt to be even closer to her?

He cleared his throat. 'Maybe Molly's got time to take Oreo in to visit Sam for a few minutes?'

'I have.' Molly nodded. 'That's why I came down. We could only be in the ICU for a very short time so we'd both appreciate a chance to make another visit.'

Annabelle lifted her face. 'Really? You could do that?'

'Why don't you go and see how Sam feels about it?' Hugh suggested. 'Come and tell us if he's awake again and his pain levels are under better control. Otherwise, it might be a bit much for him. Check with his nurse, too?'

Annabelle nodded, but an almost smile was hovering on her lips. 'Where will I find you?'

Hugh thought fast. 'I'm sure Oreo could use a breath of fresh air. We'll just be out in the garden here.'

We...?

Did Hugh want to be alone with Molly when he'd have no chance of *not* thinking—and probably saying something—about last night?

No.

Yes...

He held the door open for Molly. 'I thought you might need a bit of background,' he said quietly.

Oreo looked delighted to be back in the garden where she'd danced with Molly and, with no one else there, she could be let off the lead for a few minutes.

Molly sat on one of the benches and Hugh sat down beside her. Close enough for his thigh to be touching hers and it was inevitable that memories of last night came flooding back in a kaleidoscope of sensations that were enough to make Hugh catch his breath.

It wasn't just the sex that had been a revelation, was it? He'd never felt like this *afterwards*, either. As if his body were watching a metaphorical clock and counting down every second until he could do it again.

Molly seemed to be avoiding catching his gaze. She'd closed her eyes, in fact, and she was taking in a slow, deep breath—as if *she* were aware of that clock as well? The thought that she might be feeling the same way he was about repeating the experience was enough for Hugh to know this definitely wasn't the time to say anything. Their body language might already be enough to catch the attention of someone walking past the windows and... Hugh had no intention of turning his back on what had been disturbing enough to welcome the distraction that Molly and Oreo's arrival had provided.

'So...' His deep breath mirrored Molly's. 'Sam is four years old. I saw him about eighteen months ago when he fell off his scooter and broke his arm. His humerus. Like Sophie, the X-ray that was taken was the first indication that he had something serious going on.'

Molly's face was very still. Her eyes wide. She was absolutely focussed on what Hugh was saying. 'An osteosarcoma?' she breathed.

'No. In Sam's case it was a Ewing sarcoma. Rare. And incredibly aggressive. He had equally aggressive chemotherapy and radiotherapy and I did a limb-saving surgery to remove the diseased humerus and replace it with a bone graft that we took from his fibula.'

Molly didn't say anything when he paused for a breath this time, but Hugh could feel she was holding her own breath.

'He seemed to be doing well for some time. We thought we'd caught it. Annabelle told me she felt like she could finally breathe again. She's in her early forties. She chose to become a single mother and is totally devoted to Sam.' Hugh swallowed carefully. 'The first metastases showed up a few months ago and further chemo has been ineffective. The tumours are right through his body—in his lungs, bones, spine, brain...'

Hugh didn't bother continuing the list. 'Surgery's not an option unless it's palliative...which is why he's been transferred to my team. He broke his femur yesterday due to the bone damage from a fast-growing tumour. His leg is in a cast but it needs surgery to stabilise it effectively so I was consulted about whether removing the lesion and plating the fracture could significantly improve his level of comfort. I think it probably could but it's a much higher risk operation in his condition so it's got to be Annabelle's choice whether or not the risk is worth it. We're keeping a theatre slot free for later today, just in case.'

Hugh had been watching Oreo exploring the garden as he spoke quietly. Perhaps instinct had been protecting him from making direct eye contact with Molly, because now, when he turned his head, he could see a level of emotion in her face and eyes that he would never let himself feel for a patient.

Yes, this was an incredibly sad story and it was reaching an even sadder ending but that only made it vital for Hugh not to be sucked into an emotional vortex. He had to stand back far enough to offer support and make the best decisions for both Sam and his mum, Annabelle.

'So…' The word was crisp, this time. Decisive. 'If you—and Oreo—can handle it, it might be… you know…'

He didn't finish his sentence. It was too heartbreaking to think about a small child finding even a moment of joy in what could be his last days alive. Or a memory being made that his mother might treasure for the rest of her life. He didn't need to finish it…

'I know,' Molly whispered. She was blinking hard and then she lifted her chin. 'And it's precisely why I got into this in the first place. Oreo's at her best with children like Sam. My job is just to put her in the right place at the right time.'

Maybe Oreo heard her name. Or maybe she'd picked up on Hugh's tone of voice. She'd given up exploring and come to lie quietly at their feet. When the doors to the garden opened and Annabelle came out to find them, Oreo wasn't looking at the newcomer. She was gazing up at Molly, waiting for her cue.

And Molly looked down at her dog. It was a moment of silent communication. A warning perhaps that they were about to do something difficult but it would be okay because they would be doing it together.

It was a message carried on an undercurrent that felt like…

…like love. A love so strong it was palpable.

It was only between Molly and Oreo but, for a heartbeat, before he could definitively shut it down, Hugh felt as if he was included in it.

Or perhaps he'd just *wanted* to be…

Oh…*man*…

Emotional moments were part and parcel of

a job working with sick kids and their families. Being with a mother who was facing the final days of her precious child's life took it to a whole new level. Adding all the feels that bringing a dog into the picture could provide made it...

...poignant enough to be a pain like no other.

How much easier would it be to be able to put up a wall to protect yourself from that kind of pain—the way Hugh Ashcroft seemed to be able to do with ease? Molly hadn't heard any wobble of emotion in his voice when he'd been filling her in on Sam's case out in the garden earlier. He'd avoided looking at her as he'd given her the clinical facts. He was concerned with weighing up the benefits versus risks of a surgical procedure and making sure the mother was able to make an informed consent. Or not.

And yes...knowing that he'd lost his sister to a childhood cancer gave her an insight into why he was like he was but...but it still didn't make sense. Not when she knew that beneath the cool, professional persona that Hugh put on in public there was a man who was capable of feeling things.

Passionately feeling things...

Things you might expect like the satisfaction of saving a young life or ensuring a better future for a child.

But unexpected things, too—like the power of the ocean.

Like the sensual pleasure of the intimate touch of another human.

It had been surprisingly hurtful to find herself shut out again, so when Molly saw Hugh also heading towards the lifts from the direction of his office, she increased her pace.

'Hugh? Have you got a minute?'

He looked up from the screen of his phone and Molly's heart sank. She could swear he was dismayed to see her and Oreo.

'Is it important?'

'I think so.' Molly tried to keep her tone calm. 'I've just come from being with Sam and his mum.'

Hugh glanced at his watch. 'Really? You've been in there for more than an *hour*?'

'Sam was so happy to have Oreo there. We let her lie on the bed beside him and he went to sleep with his arm around her. We didn't want him to wake up and find she'd disappeared.'

Because Annabelle had known he would start crying instantly. From the pain he was in and because his new friend was no longer beside him.

'We got some lovely photos.' Molly pulled her phone out. 'Would you like to see them?'

'Not right now.' Hugh was turning towards the lift. 'I've got a lot to get on with.'

'You'll probably have even more soon. Anna-belle's decided that she wants Sam to have the surgery on his leg. If he gets enough analgesia to cope with the pain, he's completely knocked out.'

'Thanks for the heads-up.' Hugh was frowning now. Thinking about what might be a difficult surgery? 'Is she certain about that?'

Molly nodded. 'She said that if it could keep Sam comfortable to enjoy his favourite food or a bedtime story or even one more visit and a cuddle with Oreo, then it would be worth it.' Molly was staring at Hugh's profile. 'I've promised I'll bring her to see him every day I can, depending on my shifts. Either here, or when they get home again.'

'*If* they get home.' Hugh's words were a mut-ter that nobody nearby would have overheard. They would have heard the disapproving tone in his next words though. 'I don't think that's a good idea.'

Molly blinked. He didn't want to see the pho-tos and that was fine. She understood that images of a frail child with no hair, IV lines in his arms and oxygen tubing taped to his face could be confronting for Hugh when they had nothing to do with anything medical. But to deny that child the moments of joy—of forgetting that life could be unbearably hard—that was also so apparent in those photos was…well…it was unacceptable.

'Why not?' Molly demanded.

It wasn't surprising that the challenging note in her voice was enough for Hugh's registrar, who was stepping into the lift, to turn and stare at them. Or that Molly could see a flash of…what was it? Annoyance? Anger, even?…on Hugh's face.

'Not here,' he said coldly. 'Come with me.' He turned away from where Matthew was holding the lift door open. 'Go ahead without me,' he told him. 'I'll be there in a few minutes.'

He strode back to his office, held the door for Molly and Oreo to enter and then closed it behind them, with a decisive click.

'Sam may not survive this surgery,' he said, without preamble. 'If he does, it might make him more comfortable but it will not prolong his life. He's on palliative care and Annabelle knows that the probability is very high that he won't make it home again.'

'I'm aware of that,' Molly said.

'Are you also aware that you're at risk of getting too involved in this case? On a personal level?'

'I know what I'm doing,' Molly said. 'It's not the first time I've worked with a terminally ill child, Hugh.'

He was staring at her as if she'd just stepped off a spacecraft from another planet.

'Why?' He sounded bemused. 'I don't understand how—or *why*—you would choose to get so involved in a case like this?'

'And I don't understand how *you* can avoid it,' Molly said quietly.

Maybe that was it in a nutshell. Why they could never be together, no matter how tightly Molly's feelings for Hugh had entwined themselves around her heart.

'I *learned* how. So that I could be capable of doing my job properly, without having decisions affected by unhelpful emotional involvement with my patients *or* their families.'

Hugh met her gaze and the shutters were firmly down. It felt like Molly was being given a reprimand. That she should also do what it took to acquire this skill?

'It's better to keep an appropriate, professional distance,' Hugh added as if she had somehow agreed with his viewpoint.

She stared back. It wasn't going to happen. She wasn't even going to try and make it happen.

'Distance from what? Or whom?' she asked, enunciating her words clearly. 'Just from the patients and their families? From your colleagues?'

Like her...?

'From *life*...?' Molly forgot that she was speaking to a senior colleague, here. Or that they were in the place they needed to be able to work together in amicably, never mind what had happened between them away from the hospital. Perhaps it was the hurt caused by realising that their time together out of hours was not significant that was making her angry. That he could have sex with her and then push her away to protect that precious distance…

Hugh opened his mouth and then closed it again, clearly unable to find the words he wanted. Oreo was pressed against Molly's leg and she could feel the shiver that ran through her dog's body. She put her hand gently on Oreo's head to let her know she wasn't the one who was doing anything wrong.

'Who's it better *for*, Hugh?' Molly wasn't done yet. 'It's never going to be better for the other person, or people, in the equation. So let me answer that, if you haven't already figured it out for yourself.' She narrowed her eyes. 'It's better for *you*. And only you. Me? I'll continue to let people know how much I care about them because…in the end, that's better for *me*.'

Molly didn't give Hugh a chance to respond. She turned and walked out of his office, Oreo glued to her side.

She knew she'd crossed a rather significant boundary line but she hadn't said anything that she didn't believe in. Being distant was never going to be better for someone like Sophie Jacobs and her family. Or for Sam and his mother, who was going through unimaginable pain right now.

And yeah…keeping that kind of distance was never going to be better for herself, either. Or Oreo. Even as they reached the staircase, Oreo was looking back towards the office they'd just stormed out of. Hoping to see the man she, for some inexplicable reason, had decided she was devoted to.

Okay…maybe it wasn't inexplicable. Because Molly's heart had been equally captured, hadn't it?

And that was when Molly changed her mind. Hugh keeping this distance he'd learned to do so well *might* actually be better in this case.

For both of them.

CHAPTER EIGHT

'SO WHAT ACTUALLY HAPPENED, Tane?'

The lanky thirteen-year-old that Hugh had been called into the emergency department to see made a face that hinted at how enormous this catastrophe could be for him.

'It was the final moments of the game, bro. I had the ball and it was the only chance for us to break the tie before the whistle went. And I did the highest jump shot ever…got it through the net…crowd goes wild…but then I landed…'

'Did you hear anything go pop or feel it snapping as you landed?'

'Felt like someone shot me in the back of my foot, you know?' He had his hand shielding his eyes now. 'They had to carry me off the court.'

Tane was still wearing the boxer shorts and singlet with his number and the name of his team.

'Can you turn over so you're on your stomach?' Hugh asked. 'Hang your feet over the end of the bed…that's it. And now relax your feet and calf muscles as much as you can.' He took hold of the calf muscle above the ankle on Tane's uninjured leg, squeezed it firmly and watched the foot move downwards. The same stimulus on the other leg provoked no movement whatsoever in the foot.

'You've definitely ruptured your Achilles tendon,' Hugh told him.

'Oh, *man*... How long am I going to be out for?'

'Depends on the severity, which we'll find out when I send you for an ultrasound and an MRI scan. If it's a minor or partial tear, you'll be in a cast or walking boot for six to eight weeks. If it's severe or a complete rupture, it'll need surgery and it will take a lot longer to heal.'

'But there's a sponsors' tournament that's part of the national team's selection series next month...'

Tane was on the verge of tears so Hugh didn't tell him he thought this injury was quite likely to be on the severe end of the spectrum. Time enough to do that when the results of the scans came through. Right now, it was time for Hugh to be somewhere else. Before the tears started.

'I'll be back to see you as soon as you've had the scans done,' he said, turning away from his patient. 'We'll talk about the next steps then.'

Sometimes, it was kinder to give people the chance to prepare themselves for bad news, but if Tane needed surgery to reattach the tendon to his heel or possibly replace part of it with a graft and it was going to take six months or more to heal, then Hugh would tell him. If the lad got tearful or angry he wouldn't let it affect him on a personal level, or change whatever management he advised.

That was what keeping an emotional distance enabled him to do. And yes, it was better for Tane as well as for himself. How would it help anyone if he sat here, holding this boy's hand and sympathising with what a disaster this was for his hopes of making the national team? Or worse, letting himself be persuaded that it might be okay to try a conservative approach with a few weeks' rest in a cast first and then finding it could be harder to achieve the best result from a surgical repair.

Molly was wrong.

His complete opposite, in fact.

Hugh was at a loss to understand why he'd been attracted to her in the first place, but at least he could be confident it wasn't going to get any more complicated. From now on, he was going to keep an emotional distance from Molly Holmes as well as his patients.

Preferably, a physical distance as well.

He hadn't even gone into the induction room the other day, when he'd learned that Molly had stayed on so that Oreo could be with Sam as he was taken to Theatre and given his anaesthetic. He hadn't seen her in the ward since that surgery despite knowing that Sam had not been discharged and it was unlikely to happen as they kept the little boy comfortable in a private room away from the main bustle of the ward.

If Molly was keeping her promise and taking Oreo in to see him every day possible, perhaps she was avoiding him as well now that it was obvious they had so little in common?

Hugh should be happy that it was going to make it easy to forget the unfortunate lapses of his normal self-control that had led to doing things as outrageous as running around an agility course with a dog.

And having *sex* in a shower?

The fact that he wasn't happy and that it was proving surprisingly difficult to forget anything about Molly was enough to give Hugh a background hum of something unpleasantly reminiscent of anger. And that only made him even *less* happy.

Mr Hugh Ashcroft wasn't looking aloof when Molly saw him walking briskly past the windows when she was giving Oreo a toilet break in the roof garden.

He was looking as if he was in a decidedly bad mood.

He was actually scowling!

Thank goodness he didn't look outside and see her because that would, no doubt, make him even grumpier. They hadn't spoken since she'd unleashed on his lack of connection with his patients the other day. They hadn't even made eye contact. And...

...and Molly was missing him.

Okay, she knew perfectly well that they were totally unsuited to being with each other but that didn't change the fact that Molly's heart had been well and truly captured—even before he'd given her the best sex she'd ever had in her life.

Even now, as she saw the tall man with the scowl on his face striding past the garden, she could also see a lonely boy who had not only been grieving the loss of his sister but had lost his beloved dog as well. Molly could almost see the barriers he'd built to prevent himself feeling that much again and her heart ached for him because she knew, all too well, that those barriers were also preventing him from feeling the joy that life could offer.

She'd already pushed him too far, though, hadn't she?

She wasn't going to get another chance and that made her feel sad.

Almost as sad as she felt every time she and Oreo quietly slipped into Sam's room to spend some time with him. The sweet little boy was being kept pretty much pain free now but the complications with his lungs and heart were making his care too complex for Annabelle to be able to manage at home.

She knew she was going to be saying goodbye to her precious son in hospital within a short period of time but she was making the most of every moment she still had with him, and the way Sam's face lit up when he was conscious enough to know that Oreo was beside him was enough for Molly to make sure she came in every day. She enlisted the help of her mother one day when she was on duty to bring Oreo to the hospital to make a brief visit during Molly's lunch break and on another day she came back in the evening after she'd finished her shift.

There were many other patients needing her attention, of course.

Sophie Jacobs had gone home a week after her rotationplasty surgery. She would need crutches and a wheelchair until her leg had healed enough to be fitted for her custom-made prosthesis and she would be spending a great deal of time with her team of physiotherapists to learn to use her ankle joint as her new knee, but she left the ward with a huge smile on her face and the picture from her wall, of the other little girl doing her ballet leap with her prosthesis, folded up and in her pocket. She gave Molly a copy of one of the photographs the nurse had taken when Oreo visited Sophie in the intensive care unit after her surgery. Sophie had been just waking up and the smile on her face as she'd been able to touch Oreo's head was enough to melt anyone's heart.

Maybe even the heart of the man who'd done Sophie's surgery?

Molly pinned the photo, with pride, to a long corkboard on the wall near the entrance to the ward. She—and her beloved canine partner—were becoming a part of the fabric of this hospital and nobody—other than Hugh—had questioned the wisdom of their frequent visits to a small boy who was dying.

Molly had been invited to attend a very sombre meeting where an end-of-life care plan was discussed for Sam. Hugh was apparently caught up in Theatre but his presence wasn't considered necessary given that Sam would not be having any further surgery. His oncologist and cardiologist were there, along with Molly representing the nursing staff and the support of Sam's grandmother and aunty for Annabelle. At the end of the meeting, Annabelle signed consent forms for a process known as Allowing a Natural Death or AND, which meant keeping Sam as comfortable as possible for as long as possible but restricting the interventions to prevent death, such as CPR including intubation or defibrillation. She also made what was, for this hospital, the first request of its kind, ever.

'I know it's a lot to ask…' Annabelle's words were choked '…and maybe it won't be possible but… I think Sam believes that Oreo is *his* puppy now. If she could be there at…at the end…'

She broke down completely then and Molly was the first to get up and go to give Annabelle a hug. She knew that any comfort Oreo could provide would be for Annabelle as much as for Sam.

'If it's possible,' she said softly, 'we'll make it happen.'

It *was* a big ask. Not because Molly wasn't willing to be there if it was at short notice or in the middle of the night but because it was quite likely that Sam's heart function or respiratory efforts could cease without any warning. What did end up happening, however, was a more gentle progression with signs that Sam's small body was giving up the fight. His blood pressure dropped and his body temperature began fluctuating. His skin became slightly mottled as his circulation slowed down and Annabelle found she couldn't tempt her son to eat, even with his favourite treats.

Molly took Oreo in during the afternoon. Assistant dog protocols meant that she had to stay in the room with Annabelle, *her* mother and her

sister but, having positioned Oreo on the bed beside where Sam was being held in his mother's
arms, she made herself as inconspicuous as possible in a corner of the room. Oreo looked as
though she was asleep, with her eyes shut and
Sam's hand just resting on top of her body and
Annabelle stroking her sometimes, but, occasionally, the dog would open her eyes and her
glance would find Molly's, as if seeking reassur-
ance she was doing the right thing as she stayed
there, motionless, for an hour and then another.
And Molly would smile and sometimes murmur
quietly, telling her that she was a good girl and
to stay where she was.

Oreo still didn't move even after Sam quietly
sighed and then didn't take another breath. Molly
waited until Annabelle's mother and sister closed
in to share the holding and grieving for Sam and
then signalled Oreo, who slipped off the bed un-
noticed by the family.

The charge nurse on duty, who was in the room
at that point, followed Molly and Oreo out of the
room.

'Are you okay?' she asked Molly.

Molly could only nod. She didn't trust her
voice to work yet.

'Take Oreo home.' The charge nurse gave her
a quick hug. 'And look after yourself. You're both
heroes, you know that, don't you?'

Molly tried to smile but it didn't work. It was time for her to take Oreo home and she knew that Sam's family would be well cared for and allowed to stay with him as long as they wanted to. Her own tears were making everything a bit of a blur as she walked out of the ward, but Oreo knew the route well by now and was leading Molly towards the stairwell beside the lifts. In a few minutes they would be outside and then in the familiar privacy of the old van. Maybe she knew how important it was that Molly needed to get somewhere where she could have a good cry.

She didn't see him.

She probably wouldn't have recognised him if he'd been standing right in front of her because Hugh could see that Molly was half blinded by tears.

And he knew why.

He'd been heading towards his office when someone had intercepted him and told him quietly that little Sam Finch had died. Hugh had simply nodded acknowledgement and thanked the messenger and it was then he'd spotted Molly leaving the ward with Oreo.

There was no reason not to continue to his office, where he had an article on an experimental surgical technique for bone grafting waiting for him to peer review for a leading journal of paediatric orthopaedics.

Yes, the news was sad but it was part and parcel of specialising in orthopaedic surgery for children with bone cancer and, fortunately, they seemed to be winning more and more battles these days. Hugh had learned long ago how to protect himself from being sucked too deeply into a case like Sam's.

But Molly clearly hadn't.

A short time later, Hugh found the image of her struggling to control her grief as she escaped the hospital was interfering with his focus on the article.

Where had she gone? Was she alone in that little cottage by the sea?

Was she okay?

Did she have someone to talk to?

Someone that could help her get past what could be a damaging level of emotional involvement rather than wallowing in it?

Someone like himself...?

Hugh shook the notion off and tried harder to focus on what was a well-written paper, on the advancements in biomaterials and methods for bone augmentation, but he couldn't prevent his thoughts drifting back to Molly.

He couldn't get rid of the odd tightness in his chest that was unusual enough for him to wonder if he might have an undiagnosed issue with his heart.

No. He knew what the problem was.

He was worried about Molly. He'd warned her about how unwise it had been to involve herself in this case but that didn't mean he wasn't sympathetic to her finding out the hard way that he was right.

He wasn't going to say 'I told you so'. He wasn't expecting her to take back the things she'd said about his ability to distance himself being selfish because he was the only person to benefit and that he was living less of a life than others.

To be honest, Hugh had no idea what he was going to say or what Molly might say back to him. He just knew he needed to see her, which was why he closed his laptop and reached for his car keys.

This was better.

Molly had cried her eyes out at the same time as throwing the frisbee for Oreo again and again. The background of waves breaking on the beach was soothing and a soft evening sea breeze was enough to dry the tears on her cheeks without becoming too cold. When Oreo was panting so hard she had to drop her toy and head into the waves to cool off, Molly sat to simply watch for a while and that was even better because she could feel the edges of her sadness being softened by the comfort of being in a place she loved.

With the dog she loved with all her heart.

Oddly, it wasn't surprising to look up and see Hugh walking towards her. Molly knew that he would have heard about Sam and he'd warned her how hard it might be to have involved herself so much. But the fact he was here told her that he wasn't being judgemental or righteous because being like that would be far more effective in their working environment. His expression suggested that he was feeling concerned.

Concerned about her?

That was a kind of involvement on his part, wasn't it?

That meant he wasn't keeping himself as distant as he might think.

And, for some reason, Molly felt a spark of something that felt like…hope…?

'I thought I might find you here,' he said.

Molly just nodded.

'I thought you might like a bit of company.'

Molly nodded again and Hugh sat down on the sand beside her. For a minute or two they both watched the waves endlessly rolling in and then receding. And then Hugh spoke quietly.

'You okay…?'

Oh… Molly could hear how difficult it was for him to ask that question. He knew he was inviting a conversation that might include something emotional. Something a long way out of any comfort zone of his.

She needed to reassure him that she wasn't going to stamp on any personal ground so she managed to find a smile as she nodded slowly.

'I'm okay,' she said. 'I'm incredibly sad, of course. I'm gutted for Annabelle and her family but I don't regret my involvement. And Oreo was an absolute angel. I know she helped...'

'I'm sure she did.'

Molly had to brush away a few leftover tears. She could feel Hugh's gaze on her face and the increase of tension in his body language.

'I really am okay,' she told him. 'It's okay to feel sad sometimes, you know. And it's okay to cry...'

Oreo was still playing in the shallow water. They had the beach to themselves and the only sound was the soft wash of small waves breaking.

'I haven't cried since I was fourteen.'

Hugh's words were not much more than a whisper and Molly knew he was telling her something he had never told anyone else.

'When you lost your sister?'

Hugh was silent for so long that Molly thought she might have crossed too big a boundary but then he spoke again and his voice was raw.

'And Fudge...' The way he cleared his throat

made Molly wonder if he was close to tears himself. 'My mother had him put down a few days after Michelle died.'

Molly gasped in total shock. 'Oh, my God… what happened to him?'

Hugh was staring out to sea. 'Nothing…my mother just said he was too old. I came home from school and he…just wasn't there…'

Molly was staring at Hugh. Horrified. Imagining that boy who was dealing with the loss of his sister and having the lifelong companion who could have offered comfort like no other simply snatched away for no good reason. Her heart was breaking for fourteen-year-old Hugh. But it was also breaking for the man who was sitting beside her.

Who'd learned not to love any people—*or* dogs—because the world would feel like it was ending when you lost them.

All Molly wanted to do was to hold Hugh in her arms. To offer, very belatedly, all the understanding and comfort that *she* was able to bestow.

She knew not to touch him, however. That Hugh had stepped onto an emotional tightrope by telling her something so personal and, if he was touched in any way, verbally *or* physically, he could fall off that tightrope and she'd never be allowed this close again.

And she really didn't want that to happen.

Because it was in this moment that Molly realised just how much in love with Hugh Ashcroft she had fallen.

She knew he was never going to feel the same way. That if she didn't back off she would be setting herself up for total heartbreak but…it didn't feel like she had a choice, here. It was a bit like being with Annabelle and Sam today. There was something powerful enough to make dealing with that level of pain worthwhile.

That she—and Oreo—could help.

'I've got a spot in my garden where you can watch the sea while the sun sets,' she said, as if she were sharing something secret. Or perhaps just completely changing the subject? 'I've also got a bottle of wine in my fridge and I'd really like a glass of it but you know what they say about not drinking alone, don't you?'

Hugh nodded carefully. 'I *do*…'

'I know I'm not technically alone when I've got Oreo with me.' Molly bit her lip. And then she smiled. Properly this time. 'But she hates wine.'

The soft huff of laughter from Hugh was a surprise.

A definite win.

'I did come out because I thought you might need some company.' Hugh got to his feet and held out his hand to help Molly up. 'I didn't realise it was to drink wine but…hey… I'm willing to go with the flow, here.'

Molly put her hand in his, loving the strong grip and tug that made it so easy to get up and stay this close to Hugh.

It would have been easy to keep moving. To lean in so close it would be an invitation to be kissed.

But Molly didn't do that. Because if offering him an opportunity to get closer—to build a friendship, or even a relationship—was going to work, it had to be completely Hugh's choice how far he closed any distance between them.

Safety.

That was what this felt like.

He had been pretty sure Molly would have been filled in by Benji's grandmother about his family tragedy, but nobody had known about Fudge. That look on Molly's face when he'd dropped that emotional bomb had made him realise that this was the first time anyone understood exactly what it had been like for him.

It felt like Molly might be the only person in the universe who *could* understand that. More than understand, even. It felt like she could *feel* it herself.

And she didn't say anything. It was enough that he knew she understood. He certainly didn't want to revisit the past in any more detail and Molly seemed to get that, too.

So yeah…

Hugh felt safe. He could sit on a comfortable, old wicker chair with Oreo lying on the grass by his feet, drink a very nice Central Otago wine and still hear the waves as the day drew to a close and he could relax more than he remembered being able to do in…well…in for ever, really.

Perhaps that was why it felt okay to have Oreo's head resting heavily on his foot. Why, when he looked down and found the dog looking back up at him with those liquid brown eyes, he could feel a melting sensation deep in his chest. He didn't dare look up to where Molly was sitting, in the matching chair that was close enough to touch his, in case *she* was watching him, too.

'I was nine years old when Michelle… Shelly… got diagnosed with a brain tumour,' he said. 'She was only three so she never really remembered a life without being sick. She died at home when she was eight. Fudge stayed on the bed with her that day. He refused to get off even when I tried to take him outside for a wee. I think he knew…'

Oh, dear Lord…even mentioning that last day was taking him too close to a space he had successfully avoided for so long. He'd even managed to keep it locked away when he'd been trying to warn Molly that being with Sam at the end might have repercussions that could haunt her for life. If she said anything about Shelly now, he might lose something he could never get back.

His safe space...

'Dogs are amazing,' Molly said softly into the silence. 'They understand far more than we give them credit for and they have this astonishing ability to supply limitless, unconditional love...'

Her voice trailed away as if she felt like she'd said too much and when Hugh lifted his gaze he could see she had tears in her eyes.

'Grief is the worst feeling in the world, isn't it?' she murmured. 'I heard it said once that grief is love that has nowhere to go.'

Hugh had no words. He was lost in what he could see in Molly's dark eyes. They were sitting so close that all he had to do was lift his hand to touch her cheek. If he leaned towards her he would be able to kiss her.

Especially if she leaned a little, as well.

Which was exactly what she did a heartbeat after he'd moved. Hugh cupped her cheek with his hand, tilting her jaw as his lips found hers.

He didn't need any words, did he?

Not even to tell Molly how she had made such a difference in his world just by being there to hear him talk, even so briefly, about his beloved little sister. And his dog. To understand how devastating it had been to lose them both but not to ask him to say anything more. To allow him the dignity of maintaining control. One day he might tell her how his mother had disappeared, inch by inch, into the depression that eventually claimed her life. That *he* had largely disappeared for her over the years when her sick daughter was the total focus of her life.

But not now. All he wanted right now was to thank Molly for being here.

For understanding.

And he didn't need words.

Because he could touch her.

He could hold her face as he kissed her until they were both short of breath. He could stand up and take her hand and lead her into her little house and find her bedroom this time.

And he could touch her whole body—with his hands and his lips and his tongue. He could feel her skin against his own. He could make sure that this was as good as it could get—for both of them. And he could take his time because this was about more than simply a fierce physical attraction.

It was about being safe. In a world that only the two of them could inhabit.

Because Molly understood why he was so different.

CHAPTER NINE

As THE NURSE practitioner on duty, it was part of Molly's job to accompany the consultants and their registrars as they made their ward rounds. Prior to that, she needed to collect all the most up-to-date clinical information on the patients and be ready for the 'board round' before the ward round. This was where the team would gather around the digital whiteboard on the wall of the nurses' station, which had details of all the inpatients, and decide the order of priority. The most unwell were seen first, then the patients who were ready for discharge that day, followed by the more routine visits to everyone else for the monitoring of charts and medications, physical examinations and any adjustments to treatment plans.

It was Hugh, his registrar Matthew and two junior doctors doing their rounds this morning and Molly had been completely focussed collecting all the latest blood test results and notes from the handover, until Hugh and his colleagues walked towards the nurses' station for the board round.

Her stomach did a weird flip-flop then and, for a moment, Molly struggled to clear a sudden flash of images from her brain—like a movie on fast-forward—of last night. Of her body being… good heavens…*worshipped*…?

But that was what she had decided it had felt like later in the night, after Hugh had gone home. The focus he'd had on her… As if making this the most profound sexual experience she'd ever had was the only thing on his mind?

Maybe it wasn't images that flashed through her mind in that heartbeat of a moment. It was more like a reminder of physical sensations like none she had ever had before in her life. The sheer delight of the whispers of fingers against her skin. The delicious spears of desire. Anticipation—and need—building to a point that was actually painful and the blinding ecstasy of release.

No…it was more than that. It was like the physical form of emotions that were so intense and unfamiliar Molly couldn't even find words to describe them. And she certainly wasn't about to try right now.

This was work and Molly knew perfectly well that it came before anything else in this surgeon's list of what mattered the most. If there was a way to ensure that what had happened between herself and Hugh Ashcroft last night never, ever happened again, it would be to let it interfere with how either of them did their jobs. That deal-breaker was closely followed by putting any kind of pressure on Hugh to build on how well they knew each other, but at least that was easy to put aside, especially when Molly wasn't at all sure she was ready for even attempting a new relationship. The reminder was useful, however, because suddenly any personal thoughts evaporated.

The blip in focus had been so momentary hopefully nobody else could have noticed. Especially Hugh. Molly took a deep breath as she looked away from him and flicked open the notepad where she'd scribbled the information she needed to communicate with this team that wasn't on the whiteboard yet.

The first patient whose condition was causing some concern was twelve-year-old Gemma, who had had surgery two days ago for a slipped upper femoral epiphysis—where the ball at the top of the femur had slipped out of position due to damage to the growth plate—that had happened after a collision and fall in a soccer game.

'So, Gemma was doing very well with her crutches and was flagged for discharge today but she spiked a temperature during the night and is feeling unwell this morning,' Molly reported. 'She's got some redness and is complaining of increased wound pain. Preliminary results on the bloods and wound swab I took first thing after handover shouldn't be too far away.'

'Thanks, Molly. Is the ward pharmacist available? I'd like to run through our initial management of any infection.'

'I'll get someone to page her.'

Hugh's glance told her that he was impressed with her initiating tests that would determine the course of treatment needed to combat the surgical complication of infection.

It also told her that they were both now safely in a totally professional arena. That Hugh had no idea of that momentary lapse she'd had. But perhaps he hadn't been entirely wrong in telling her it was better to be able to keep a personal distance from others. Sometimes.

Like for the rest of this ward round. With Gemma examined, antibiotic treatment started and her family reassured that she wouldn't be discharged until this setback had been sorted, there were enough patients to keep the team busy until it was time for a morning tea break. Not that Hugh or his team stayed for a coffee in the ward staff room. They were gone, heading towards Radiology for a scheduled biopsy, a family meeting in the oncology ward for a patient who had just been diagnosed with a bone cancer and was about to start chemotherapy before surgery, and then an outpatient clinic that was apparently so packed it would keep both himself and his registrars largely unavailable all afternoon.

'I know you won't page us unless it's urgent,' he said to Molly as they left the ward.

She might have deemed the smile she received to be as aloof as she'd once thought Hugh actually was himself, but she could see past that protective barrier now. Or maybe it was just something new she could see in that graze of eye contact. Something that acknowledged there was a lot more than simply being colleagues between them but that Hugh was trusting her with much more than overseeing the care of his patients for the rest of her shift.

He was trusting her not to trespass across boundaries.

Especially at work, because this was his safe place.

Molly's smile in return was just as polite. 'Of course not,' she murmured.

He *could* trust her. On both counts. He'd never know that she had a totally *un*professional thought as he walked away from her. That, as she carried her mug of coffee out to the garden for a minute's peace and quiet, she was reminded—oddly—of a pony club camp she'd been to as a teenager, taken by a local legend in horse whispering.

At first Molly couldn't understand why her

brain had dredged up something she hadn't thought about in more years than she could count.

'Every horse lives with a mindset that's like a human with PTSD,' she remembered the course leader saying to them as he gave them a demonstration. *'They have eyes on the sides of their heads. They've always been prey, not the predators. They're hypervigilant. Always looking for danger...'*

Molly found herself catching her breath, as she slowly sat down on a bench and put her coffee down beside her. That was Hugh as far as relationships went, wasn't it? Hypervigilant. A kind of prey because a relationship was something that could hurt him. Destroy him, even.

The emotional trauma from his childhood must have left huge scars. Remembering what he'd told her about his baby sister's last day alive brought a lump to her throat that was sharp enough to be painful as she imagined how terrible that day must have been for a boy and his dog.

And how hard had those five years before that day been? All the attention would have been on the sick little girl to start with. Had that become a way of life? Had Hugh been left feeling abandoned? Molly had the odd urge to reach back through time and give that boy a hug. To make sure he knew how important he was, too. That he knew he was loved.

The unbearable heartache of losing Fudge before he'd even had a chance to process the loss of his sister was unthinkable.

So yeah…it wasn't a crazy analogy that he was like the horse running around the edges of that round pen with the trainer standing in the centre. That Hugh had learned to keep that distance from any kind of relationships that the trainer represented.

But he'd circled closer to Molly, hadn't he? Close enough to tell her a little bit about that childhood trauma. Close enough to make love to her, even if he hadn't realised that was what it was.

Just the way that horse had circled closer to the trainer when it had had time to read the signals, accept the newcomer in its life and trust that this person wasn't a threat.

'Then you can turn your back and walk away and the horse will come up behind you.' The trainer had slowed and then stopped and the horse had nudged his shoulder. *'Now I can walk away and the horse gets to choose where he wants to be and…look…he's right behind me. He wants to be with me…'*

Good grief…it was time to stop this before it got silly. Before Molly could imagine Hugh following her around like some sort of lovestruck puppy. Her coffee was too cold to be desirable now so she tipped it out into the garden behind her and stood up. It was time she went back to work now, anyway.

She did feel more at peace, she realised. She'd already known instinctively that Hugh needed the time and space to make his own choices. He'd already come close enough for it to be meaningful and that was…

…it was huge.

And very, very special.

Molly could wait. If anything else was going to happen between them, it would be well worth waiting *for*.

Working together made things so much easier.

If Hugh didn't see Molly at work, either when she was on duty or there with Oreo to visit sick kids and sometimes with Milo as a training exercise, the pressure might have been unwelcome.

It would certainly have been unforgivable not to make contact with her after the evening of the day that little boy, Sam, had died. When he'd opened a door into his personal life that was never opened to anyone—even to himself, if he could avoid it. The evening that had included sex that had been somewhat disturbing in its level of intimacy.

Not that Molly had given any hint of it being a problem for her. That next morning, when they'd met in the ward, had made it seem like it was no big deal. That it could have been simply an evening with a friend that had happened to end up in bed. That she didn't necessarily expect it to happen again and definitely wasn't going to let it impinge on their professional relationship.

Gemma, who'd had the unfortunate complication of a nasty post-op infection, had needed a bit more time in hospital to get it under control and for her to then catch up on the skills she needed with her crutches before she could go home but she'd been discharged yesterday. It was during that ward round, when Hugh had signed off on the discharge, that he'd realised how easy this was.

It felt like he and Molly were friends now. Even better, that there was no pressure for it to be anything more than that. He didn't have to ask her out on a formal date or anything but he didn't have to avoid her company, either, and that was a relief.

He didn't have to give up on one of his favourite beaches to go and catch a wave. With the days getting longer and the weather more reliable, Hugh was hoping to get into the sea as often as his work schedule would allow. Because there was nothing better than surfing to escape… well…everything, really.

Except…maybe there was *one* thing better than surfing.

And, as the days ticked past and the smiles and quick chats, when his path crossed with Molly's, became something familiar and welcome, Hugh was starting to wonder if she might like to spend some more personal time together again.

He didn't want to ask because that might make it seem more significant than he wanted it to be. And, anyway, hadn't all the time they'd had together happened without any prior arrangements? When he'd discovered her in the outpatient department with Milo after hours and ended up helping with the young dog's training. When he'd taken that old equipment out to her house and ended up running around the agility course with Oreo. When he'd gone to the beach for a breath of fresh air and ended up swimming in sea that was so cold he'd needed that hot shower and…

Hugh blew out a breath. If he went too far down that mental track he might get lost in a level of desire that could ring alarm bells. But was there a theme here? He'd gone to find Molly on the beach the day Sam had died.

He'd met her away from work for the first time on that beach, come to think of it. Maybe all he needed to do was head for Taylors Mistake again to find out what fate had in store for him?

Whether Molly *did* want more of what had

happened the last time he'd gone in that direction? No pressure, of course. On either side. And definitely no strings attached either.

No...

It couldn't be.

Which was a silly thing to think because this was exactly where she'd met Hugh Ashcroft more than once and, like the very first time, he was wearing his skintight wetsuit again and that was enough to know exactly who he was given that Molly was taken straight back to that first wave of the sexual attraction she had felt for this man. The one that had been powerful enough to make her stomach curl and her knees weak.

Both Oreo and Milo had recognised him as well and were running towards the figure with the surfboard slung under his arm but the curl in Molly's gut this time felt very different from a wash of attraction.

It felt more like...trepidation...?

It felt as though he was walking right into the middle of her life this time.

Which, in a way, he was. The Holmes family was celebrating the birthday of Molly's niece, eight-year-old Neve. Christchurch had turned on one of its spring evenings that felt far more like summer so they were all on the beach, including the dogs, having some playtime with the chil-

dren before going back to the house for a barbecue dinner.

Molly was sitting on the sand, making castles
by filling a moulded bucket and turning it upside
down so that her youngest niece could flatten it
with a toy spade. She paused, with the bucket in
mid-air, as she took in the moment Hugh recognised the dogs and then realised she was part of
this family group.

Even from this distance, she could feel the eye
contact.

She could feel how torn he was and that made
it feel like this was a very significant moment.

A make-or-break kind of moment?

Hugh had obviously come to do some surfing
but it was quite possible—probable, even—that
he'd been hoping that he would find her here.
Molly's heart sank as she wondered if this was
the moment she'd been waiting patiently for—
when Hugh felt safe enough to make the choice to
be with her because it was something he wanted
as much as she did?

Would this be the end of any such opportunity?
Hugh was cautious enough of a one-on-one relationship. Would the dynamics of a whole family
be his worst nightmare? Molly could understand,
all too easily, why he was taken aback. He was
probably considering turning back to the car park
and escaping but she knew he wouldn't do that.

How much courage had Hugh had, as a child, to face up to what life had thrown at him?

He'd learned to get through anything, no matter how hard it was.

And he'd learned to do it alone.

Molly's heart took another dive. Not just because it was aching for someone who possibly didn't even know how much it helped to *not* be alone when facing the tough stuff in life, but because Hugh didn't know the worst of what he was walking into right now. He didn't yet have any idea that her niece was celebrating her birthday.

Her eighth birthday.

Neve was now the same age as Hugh's sister, Michelle, had been when she died…

Molly got to her feet, knocking over the half-filled sandcastle bucket in her haste. The toddler beside her waved her toy spade.

'More…' she demanded. 'Aunty 'olly…*more*…'

But Molly was walking towards Hugh.

'Oreo… *Milo*…stop harassing Hugh…'

Her brother, Jack, paused in his cricket game with his son. 'You know this guy?'

'Friend of mine from work.' Molly smiled. 'And an ace surfer. You'll be impressed. Hugh, this is my brother, Jack. I think I told you how keen on surfing he used to be.'

Jack grinned at Hugh. 'Wish I could join you out there, mate. There're some awesome waves but we haven't even finished our first innings, have we, Liam?' He turned back to the impatient boy standing with his bat in front of the plastic wickets stuck into the sand. 'Come and have a beer with us when you're done.'

Molly's mother had come to get Milo and she didn't wait for an introduction.

'I'm Jill, Molly's mum. And this is Neve. It's her birthday today.'

'I'm *eight*,' Neve announced proudly.

Hugh's gaze flew to Molly's, as if he couldn't help checking to see if she remembered the significance of this. She tried to hold his gaze. To send a silent message.

I know, Hugh... I know exactly how hard this is and I'm sorry...

But Hugh was breaking the eye contact too soon. Before the most important thing Molly wanted him to know.

You don't have to do this alone. I'm here... and... I love you...

Hugh was oblivious. He was smiling at Neve. That distant kind of smile that he used with his young patients. It didn't mean he didn't care.

It meant he knew what could happen when you cared *too* much.

'Happy birthday,' he said. 'I hope you have a wonderful party. Maybe I'll be able to see all those candles on your cake from out on the waves.'

And, with that, he excused himself with another smile and strode off into the sea.

The waves *were* awesome.

It was close to a high tide and, as often happened close to sunrise or sunset, there was a decent swell and the offshore breeze was enough to smooth things out. Best of all, the swell was on an angle so that the wave was peeling off instead of breaking all at once.

Hugh wasn't the only surfer making the most of the fading daylight but it was far from crowded, in the sea or on the beach. Molly's family celebration was, by far, the biggest group of people and Hugh was acutely aware of them each time he finished a ride and prepared to paddle back out to find another wave.

He could see Jack playing cricket with Liam and even heard the little boy gleefully shout *'Howzat?'* having presumably bowled his father out. He could see Molly building sandcastles with a toddler who was happily knocking them down with her small, red spade and, after a later wave, he saw her taking the youngest child into the shallow foam of the waves to wash the sand off her hands. The birthday girl ran to join them and they both took a hand of the toddler, lifting her up to jump the foamy curl of a spent wave.

Hugh could hear the shrieks of excitement from the baby and he recognised both Molly's laughter and Oreo's happy barking.

He saw them gathering up the toys and towels and wending their way back to the family's holiday house. He knew he would be welcomed if he chose to join them in the garden for a drink. They were probably going to start cooking sausages on the barbecue and, at some point, a cake with burning candles would appear for Neve to make her birthday wish.

But Hugh paddled back to catch another wave.

And another.

The other surfers left. Daylight was almost gone and, despite the wetsuit, Hugh was getting really cold.

He told himself that each wave would be the last one but then he decided to try just one more...

Because he wanted it to be dark enough when he got out that Molly wouldn't notice him leaving.

She knew too much and he didn't want to be at her niece's birthday party and feel her understanding. Her sympathy. To know that she genuinely cared about how he was feeling. He needed some distance.

And Molly needed it too, even if she didn't realise that.

She was in the place she needed to be. With the people—and animals—she loved so much. With her whole family and those gorgeous children who loved her back. This would be Molly's future, wouldn't it? The heart and soul of a new branch of the family with the chaos of kids and dogs and big celebrations for every birthday and Christmas.

It was never going to be Hugh's future.

How hard had it been to walk into that family scene?

Molly had known that it would be another blow to any defence mechanism he had honed to learn that it was Neve's eighth birthday. That he would be reminded of Michelle. Getting to know Oreo had been enough of a pull back into his past. To where he and Fudge had been an inseparable team. They'd both adored Michelle and had been so protective of her. They'd both comforted each other on the darker days.

There were splashes of sea water getting into his eyes and blurring his vision as he flipped out of the end of the wave and dropped onto his board to paddle back out. Or were they tears?

Hugh wasn't sure. What he was sure about, however, was that he'd come closer than he'd re-alised to losing any of the hard-won protection he'd built for himself in the years since Michelle had died. Seeing Molly with the children in her extended family was sounding a warning that he couldn't ignore. This might be his last chance to avoid any more echoes of a pain he never wanted to experience again.

And maybe Molly had been right and he *was* creating a distance from living a life that was totally fulfilling.

Maybe it *was* only better for himself.

She'd made it so very clear that she would never want to live *her* life like that.

They were complete opposites and getting close to Molly Holmes was…well…he'd always known how dangerous it was. But it had been a risk he'd been—almost—willing to take. Until now, when he could see it might be dangerous for Molly as well as himself and he couldn't allow that to happen.

Because *he* cared about her.

One day, she would be grateful for him keeping them both safe.

CHAPTER TEN

THE SAME BUT DIFFERENT.

That was how Molly began to describe the relationship she had with Hugh Ashcroft to herself as the days slid past after that family gathering on the beach to celebrate Neve's birthday.

The day that she wished had ended so very differently.

If only they could have met on the beach with nobody else there to complicate things. Or Hugh had come and knocked on her door after he'd been surfing and they could have gone for a walk in the hills with Oreo or shared a glass of wine and watched the sunset.

As Molly replayed that evening in her head time and time again, adding the fantasy of what she'd wished had happened, it always ended up with the same kind of love making as last time. The kind that had taken everything to a completely new level and made Molly realise how much she wanted to take the next step towards

a relationship that could change both their lives
and give them a future.

Together.

But it hadn't happened like that and Hugh had
obviously seen enough to make him back away
and Molly just knew it was about her family.

About the children in her life.

He'd only ever seen her interacting with the
children she worked with and their patients were
part of the professional life she shared with Hugh.
He'd never seen her with the children who were
such an important part of her personal life—and
always would be. Had it made him think that
Molly saw children of her own as part of her future? Had Hugh ever got close enough to think
about a permanent relationship with someone and
imagine creating a family of his own? Had he
made his mind up at that point that it was never
going to happen? Like the way he'd decided he
never wanted to have another dog?

She couldn't blame him for making the choices
he had in life, but it did make her feel sad.

Maybe Hugh didn't see how good he was with
kids? Or dogs, for that matter. Or that both children and dogs were instinctively drawn to him?

He was currently with fifteen-month-old Jasper, on their ward round, who was due to be discharged after the surgery he'd had on a badly
dislocated and fractured elbow.

The adventurous toddler, who'd managed to climb onto a kitchen chair and then fall onto his outstretched arm, was now in a long arm cast with his elbow fixed at a ninety-degree angle but it didn't seem to be bothering him. He was grinning up at Molly as she stood beside his mother and he was trying to lift the heavy cast on his arm so that he could reach for the stethoscope she had hanging around her neck, attracted by the bright green, plastic frog head clipped to the top of its disc.

'Can I borrow that for a sec?' Hugh asked. 'Could be just what the doctor ordered for checking the range of movement and capillary refill of those fingers.'

Molly handed him the stethoscope and Jasper's gaze followed the frog's head as it got closer.

'Ribbit-ribbit,' Hugh growled.

Hugh's registrar exchanged a grin with Molly. 'We learn that in medical school,' he said.

'True,' Hugh agreed, but he didn't look up to catch Molly's gaze.

He was watching Jasper's fingers move as he played with the frog and then he quickly checked limb baselines like skin temperature and colour. Jasper's frown as he pressed a fingernail to check blood flow suggested that his ability to feel touch was not compromised, but he didn't start crying.

Instead, the frown turned to a grin as he caught the frog and he gave a gurgle of laughter.

He liked this surgeon.

Yeah... Kids and dogs could sense things that people might not even know about themselves, couldn't they?

And yes, she could totally understand where his wariness of choosing to have a child—or a dog—of his own came from but wouldn't it be easier to accept having the joy of them in his life when they were someone else's? Molly had seen Hugh patting and playing with her dogs. He would be just as good with nieces and nephews and, in time, he might even be very grateful to have them in his life.

'I'm happy for him to go home.' Hugh nodded at Jasper's mother. 'You'll get outpatient appointments and we'll be looking at removing the cast and pins at around the four-week mark.'

'Are there any long-term complications we should be worried about? I've heard that elbows can be tricky with all the nerves and things in there.'

'I don't think you need to worry.' Hugh was trying to gently prise the disc of his stethoscope from a small but determined fist. 'There may be some limitation in the range of movement but we'll encourage him to work through that as soon as he's out of the cast. Elbows are the most complex joint in the human body and we're very careful about them because of how important they are for arms and hands to function but, if there *were* any long-term complications, like disruption to the ulnar nerve, perhaps, we can deal with them.' He smiled at the anxious mother. 'And there's no point worrying about crossing bridges like that when we may never get anywhere near them. Let's take it one step at a time and be happy that Jasper's doing very well so far.'

They moved on to the next patient on their ward round but Hugh got distracted on the way by the arrival of a new patient who was waiting by the reception desk.

'Michael… I'll come and see you later today. You've got a few appointments for things like a chest X-ray and blood tests to make sure we tick all the boxes before your surgery tomorrow. How did your exams go at school?'

'Good…'

'I'll bet you smashed them. We'll talk later, okay?'

Molly had been expecting the arrival of this teenager, who was being admitted for the surgery scheduled to correct his spinal scoliosis that was affecting his breathing. She also knew that when the surgeon visited later, he would be talking about what was going to happen tomorrow. The prospect of having bone grafts and metal rods and screws being put into his body to fuse his spine had to be terrifying, no matter how brave a face this lad was showing to the world right now. Michael's mother was certainly looking as if she was on the verge of tears as they waited to finish the admittance process paperwork.

'Hi, Michael.' Molly paused to smile at him. 'I'm Molly and I'm one of the nurses who'll be looking after you while you're with us.' She lowered her voice as if she were imparting a secret. 'I've earmarked the best bed for you. You'll get a great view of all the helicopters landing and taking off from the helipad on the next-door roof.'

'Cool.'

Michael's smile was tentative but at least it was there. Hugh had seen it as well and it felt like he had deliberately kept his head turned for long enough to catch Molly's gaze and send a private message of appreciation for her attention to his new patient.

And that ability to communicate silently was something else that was different even though they were still the same colleagues. Their opinion of each other had also changed and grown into something completely different from initial impressions. They were now people who could work together with genuine respect that was personal as well as professional. Trust had been established.

In fact, they knew each other *too* well to be considered simply friends, but it was a grey area when nothing had actually been said and Molly had no idea whether Hugh even wanted to see her again. She was, in fact, on the point of giving up her patient wait for Hugh to come and find her out of working hours.

It felt as if that initial distance between them that had become the most different aspect of their relationship was being reinstated.

Slowly but surely.

With kindness. The way someone who was so good with kids and dogs might approach something that needed to be done but could be hurtful.

Someone who'd make a great father even though he never wanted to have his own children.

Someone who had probably been the best big brother in the entire world to a little girl whose heartbreaking life was the reason he never wanted to have his own children.

And okay… Molly had been trying to follow the advice Hugh had just given Jasper's mother in taking things one step at a time and being happy with how well it was going but…

…that bridge was right there in front of her and she couldn't ignore it.

Because her heart was already aching and it would be completely broken if—or when—she had to cross the bridge that might be the only way out of a dead end.

She wasn't quite there yet, mind you. And the possibility of discovering a detour came into her head as she saw Hugh walking away having signed Jasper's discharge paperwork.

What if Hugh knew that not having children of her own was not a dealbreaker as far as a relationship with him was concerned?

And, yeah…that had been a dream once but, by the time she'd moved back to New Zealand, she'd already made peace with the possibility that it would never happen, hadn't she? She'd decided that she could be happy with the children she had in her life through her family and her work. That the fur children she would always have at home would be enough.

Perhaps she just needed to find a way to let him know that? A way that didn't put any pressure on Hugh, of course, because that would send her straight across that bridge she really, really didn't want to cross.

He heard the sound of her voice before he'd turned the corner to where the reception area bridged the two main corridors in the ward.

'Show me again…? Oh, *wow*…look at you.'

Hugh could hear the smile in her words and he knew exactly what Molly's face would look like—lit up with genuine warmth that brought a glow to everyone around her. He could feel himself taking a deeper breath, his muscles tensing, as if they could form the forcefield he needed to not feel that glow.

Because it made him remember that Molly had implied he was missing out on life by keeping himself closed off and he suspected that that glow might be one of the things he was going to miss most about not allowing himself to get too close to her.

He was somewhat blindsided, however, when he did turn the corner to find who Molly was praising with so much enthusiasm. Sophie Jacobs, wearing a cute beanie with pompom ears, was standing in front of her on her crutches and, for a split second, Hugh's head was full of the image of Molly and her dog dancing for the little girl and every cell in his body was trying to remind him of how attracted he'd been to her.

He knew he would remember the physical connection they'd discovered for the rest of his life. That he was almost certainly never going to experience anything quite like that ever again.

Sophie almost looked like she was trying to dance herself, on those crutches, but then Hugh realised that was demonstrating the range of movement she had now that she was free of her plaster cast.

'And I can do it sideways, Molly…look… I can play a game where I can hit a ball with my foot. But sometimes I just lie on a mat on the floor when I do it. It's called a hip ah…ad…'

'A hip adduction,' Hugh supplied as he came up behind Molly. 'That's great, Sophie. Do you remember to keep your heel knee pointing straight up when you do that exercise on your back?'

Sophie nodded. 'And when I walk with my crutches, I have to have it pointing in front of me like it's a torch and it's shining a light for me to see where to go.'

'That's a good way to think of it.' Molly nodded. 'Did your physio give you that idea?'

'Yes. His name's Tom and he's really nice. I'm going to physio almost every day now that I've got my brace and we're going to go swimming soon when my scars are properly joined up.'

'When did you get the cast off?'

'Last week.' It was Hugh who responded. 'I saw Sophie in Outpatients that day.' He looked around. 'Where's Mummy?'

'She went to get a coffee. Molly said I could stay with her until she gets back. We're going to see somebody else after that. The man who's making my new leg that will be like the one the dancing girl has.'

'Your prosthesis?'

'Yes… I can't say that word.' But Sophie's smile

was stretching from ear to ear. 'I can't wait…it feels like Christmas…'

Hugh found his own smile was feeling oddly wobbly and he knew that Molly was watching him. He could feel the touch of her gaze on his face but it felt as if she could see way deeper than that—as if she could see how much this child's happiness was touching his heart.

'I'd better go,' he said briskly. 'I've got a patient to see who had a big operation on his back a couple of days ago.'

'Michael's looking forward to seeing you,' Molly told him. 'He wants to ask you about when he can go home. He's been in and out of bed three times already today.'

Hugh stepped towards the desk to ask for Michael's notes.

'Want to see some more of my exercises, Molly?'

'I sure do. I might even see you in the gym this week. I take Oreo in to help children with their exercises sometimes and her friend Milo is going to start soon, too.'

'Have you got *two* dogs?'

Hugh had to wait for the ward clerk, Debbie, to find Michael's notes so there was no distraction from Sophie's excited question that was an echo of one that Hugh had asked himself that day he'd found Molly in Outpatients with both Oreo and Milo and he'd been persuaded to help with training the younger dog.

'I do,' Molly told Sophie. 'Let me show you a photo of him. He's really fluffy and he's got lot of spots.'

Hugh could see her scrolling for photos on her phone. 'Here we go… This was when Milo and Oreo were at the beach last night. They found a stick they both wanted so they decided to share and, look…they're each holding one end of it…'

'Aww… They're so *cute*…' Sophie sighed.

'I'm so proud of them,' Molly said. 'They're my fur kids.'

'Best kind to have.' Debbie grinned as she handed Michael's notes to Hugh.

'Absolutely,' Molly agreed. 'The only kind *I* really need.'

There was something in Molly's voice that made Hugh look up from where he'd flicked the notes open. She didn't look up from her phone as she kept scrolling. 'Let me find some of my mum's puppies to show you, Sophie.'

'I want a puppy,' Sophie said. 'Do you have a dog at home, Mr Ashcroft?'

'No.' Hugh closed the patient file and took a deep breath. He was still trying to identify what it was in Molly's tone that had sounded like…

What…? A warning bell…?

She needed to know, didn't she? That he couldn't give her what was going to make her happy.

Ever.

This might be the perfect opportunity to let Molly know that. Before it went any further and someone—i.e. *Molly*—got hurt. And perhaps he could do it in a way that would make it her choice as well as his own to avoid spending any more time together out of work hours.

Sophie was making it easy.

'Why not?' she asked. 'Why don't you like dogs?'

'I do like dogs,' he told her. 'But only when they're someone else's. I just don't want to live with any. I spend way too much time at work so it wouldn't be fair on them, would it?'

'But...'

Sophie's eyes were wide. She couldn't understand.

Molly could. Hugh could sense that by the way she had become so still. Pretending to be so focussed on her phone but he could tell she wasn't looking at anything in particular. She was simply avoiding looking at him.

She probably needed some time to let his words sink in and Hugh was only too happy to provide it. He walked away without a backward glance.

Maybe he needed a bit of time, too.

CHAPTER ELEVEN

A DEALBREAKER.

There was no getting past that.

It didn't matter how much in love with Hugh she was. Being prepared to forgo having her own children didn't make enough of a difference, either.

Molly simply couldn't imagine not having dogs in her life. *And* in her home.

Which meant that there was no future for her and Hugh Ashcroft.

Maybe they could be friends. Eventually. They might even laugh about it over a wine or two at some staff function in a distant future.

'I had such a crush on you back in the day, Hugh...'

'Did you? You must have known it could never have worked.'

'Yeah...we both dodged a bullet, didn't we?'

'Well... I wouldn't say that, exactly, but look at you... Happily married and with those gorgeous kids of yours—and all those dogs!'

'And look at you, Hugh. Still alone...'
'Just the way I like it. Cheers, Molly...'

Molly's breath was expelled in something that sounded like a growl. Flights of conversational imagination weren't ever going to help. If anything, they had contributed to how difficult it had been for Molly to deal with the aftermath of what had felt like a significant break-up. Which was ridiculous, really. How could she have allowed herself to get in that deep when it hadn't even been a real relationship?

Except, it had been, hadn't it?

On her side, at least.

There was nothing fake about how she'd fallen in love with Hugh.

And something told her that, even if he hadn't realised it, the attraction on Hugh's side had to have been more than purely a physical thing.

They'd connected on a level on which she just knew Hugh had never connected with anyone else.

He'd told her about his sister.

About Fudge.

They'd made love.

There hadn't been any distance at all between them that night. Every touch had been as full of an emotional connection as much as anything physical. But now, the distance between herself and Hugh felt even further than it had been the first time she'd met the aloof surgeon in the radiology procedure room. Because of how close they'd been that night, the barrier between them felt...

...impenetrable, that was what it was.

Not that the solidity of that barrier mattered when neither of them were going to make any attempt to break through it because there was no point. For both of them, what lay on the other side was not something they wanted in their future and there was no compromise that could make it work.

Molly hadn't been pushed to cross that bridge to walk—yet again—into her future alone. She had chosen to cross it because she realised that the road she'd been on with Hugh had been a dead end all along.

And she was going to be okay.

She'd spent as much time as she could playing with Bella's adorable litter of pups in the few weeks since then and she'd poured hours into stepping up Milo's training as he settled in to living with her and Oreo in the beach cottage. They all spent time walking in the hills or on the beach every day but, while there were more and more surfers there when there were some decent waves, Hugh had clearly crossed Taylors Mistake off his list of preferred beaches.

Milo was living up to his promise to become

a valuable assistance dog and would graduate to being in work rather than training on his visits to the hospital, but it was Oreo who was by her side when Molly headed for the ground floor of a wing of Christchurch Children's Hospital that was becoming one of their regular destinations.

The state-of-the-art physiotherapy department included a full-sized indoor basketball court suitable for wheelchair rugby to be played and a gymnasium crowded with exercise equipment and soft mats, walking tracks with rails on either side and even a small staircase. It also had a twenty-five-metre heated swimming pool with hoists and waterproof equipment that could cater for any level of disability. Community groups and staff members had access to some of the facilities, like the basketball court and pool, outside normal hours but Molly and Oreo weren't here today to take advantage of that privilege.

They were here to be a part of Sophie's first session of learning to walk with the custom-made prosthesis that she'd been anticipating with such excitement because it would represent a big step on her long journey back to being able to dance. Oreo took no notice of the children in wheelchairs and on beds who were working around the edges of the gymnasium. She was heading straight towards the small girl sitting at one end of a walking track with a small cluster of people around her.

'Hey, Sophie…'

'Oreo…'

Sophie's mum stepped to one side to allow Oreo to get close to Sophie's wheelchair to say hullo. Her smile was apologetic.

'We're happy to see you too, Molly—not just Oreo.'

'I'm happy that I'm allowed to be here *with* Oreo,' Molly responded. 'How exciting is this?'

Tom, the physiotherapist, was helping one of the technicians from the prosthetic department to encourage Sophie to push her foot into the first version of the artificial lower leg that would enable her to walk without needing her crutches.

That would, hopefully one day, enable her to dance again.

Sophie's face was scrunched into lines of deep uncertainty, though. Disappointment, even?

'It feels…weird…'

'It'll take a bit of getting used to.' Tom nodded. 'This is just a try on to see how it fits. And it's just your training leg so it doesn't have the brace that will fit around the top of your leg.'

Sophie's head bent further as she stared down at the leg.

'Her hair…' Molly whispered to Joanne. 'Look at those gorgeous curls coming through.'

'I know.' Sophie's mum had tears in her eyes but she was smiling. 'It's like her baby hair used to be. So soft...'

Sophie lifted her head and she was smiling now, too. 'My new foot's got a shoe the same as my other leg.'

'Of course,' Tom said. 'You can always do that with your shoes.'

'Even ballet shoes?'

'Even ballet shoes,' Tom agreed. 'Like in that picture you showed me. Now...let's see if you can stand up, sweetie.'

Sophie looked suddenly fearful but, with a determination that brought tears to Molly's eyes as well as Joanne's, she let herself be helped up to stand on her normal foot and then, very tentatively, put some weight onto the artificial foot. Then she let go of Tom's hands and held onto the rails of the walking track instead.

'Do you feel ready to take a step?' Tom asked.

Sophie shook her head. Her bottom lip wobbled.

Molly quietly signalled Oreo, who moved to where she pointed, going under the rail to sit on the track a short distance from Sophie.

'Do you want to give Oreo a treat?' Molly asked.

Sophie nodded.

Molly took a tiny piece of dried beef from the

pouch on her belt. She put it on top of the rail just out of reach for Sophie.

'Oreo really wants that treat,' she said. 'But she's not allowed to have it unless you give it to her. One step will just about get you there.'

Sophie stared at the treat. Then she looked at Oreo, who had her mouth open and her tongue hanging out and her ears down. She was smiling at Sophie. Encouraging her.

And everybody held their breath as she moved her prosthetic leg in front of her, put some of her weight onto it and then moved her other leg. She could stretch out her hand now and pick up the treat.

'It's for you, Oreo,' she said proudly. 'You're a good girl…'

'Take it nicely,' Molly reminded her dog. Not because Oreo needed reminding but because she needed to take a breath and say something so that she didn't end up with tears rolling down her face at the joy of seeing Sophie—quite literally—taking her first step into a new future.

Giving up her free time to do something like this was no hardship.

It was, in fact, inspirational and Molly knew she could channel this little girl's determination and courage to move on with her own life. She would get over missing seeing him at the beach or remembering what it had been like to have him touch her. She would learn to respect his boundaries and have no more than a polite friendship at work. There was no point in continuing to feel grief of losing what could have been with Hugh Ashcroft because it had never really been there in the first place, had it?

It took two people to want a future with each other.

Maybe her imaginary conversation with Hugh hadn't been that far off base, either. It wasn't beyond belief that she could still meet someone who would want to share her life and her dreams of a family of her own—dogs included—but, if that didn't happen, it was up to her to make sure her life was as full of joy as possible.

And, with moments like this in it, how could it not be?

Despite the fact that the physiotherapy department became like a second home for many of his patients during their rehabilitation, there was no need for Hugh Ashcroft to go into that wing of this hospital. He was very familiar with what went on in the department and he could follow up the progress his patients were making after their orthopaedic surgery by reading reports written by the physiotherapists or speaking to these experts when they attended team meetings in the ward. What was most satisfying, however, was simply observing the changes in his patients for himself during their follow up outpatient appointments.

He had to smile when he saw the way Michael was walking into the consulting room, only weeks after his spinal fusion to correct the scoliosis. Even better, the teenager had a grin that was shy but still enough to light up his face.

'Look at you,' Hugh said as he got to his feet. 'I don't think I need to ask how you're doing.'

Michael's mother looked just as happy. 'He's taller than I am now.'

Hugh clipped the X-ray films to the light boxes on the wall. 'Everything's healing very well. Look, you can see how straight things are now and where the fusion is happening between the discs in your spine. Let's get your shirt off and get you on the bed so I can have a good look at your back.'

His examination was thorough but he stopped towards the end when Michael winced.

'Does that hurt?'

'A bit.'

'Your body is having to adjust to the change in the position of your ribs. You'll find there are bits that hurt, like here in your shoulder, that didn't used to be a problem. It'll get better. Is the paracetamol enough for pain relief now?'

'Yes.'

Hugh scribbled in Michael's notes as he got dressed again and then came to sit in front of the desk with his mother beside him. 'How has the gentle exercise programme they gave you been going at home?'

'Okay.' Michael nodded.

'He gets frustrated at how tired he gets,' his mother added.

'Don't forget you've had a big surgery,' Hugh told him. 'It can take longer than you expect to recover from a general anaesthetic and blood loss. There's a lot going on in that body of yours that isn't just adjusting to a new shape—like the healing around the implants that you can see on the X-rays. That sucks up some of your energy. There are things you can't see, as well. It's a lot more work for the muscles in your trunk to be holding up a spine that's suddenly straighter and longer and that takes more energy than it used to. It's really important to pace yourself and rest as often as you need to. Full recovery can take anywhere from six to twelve months.'

'Can I start driving lessons during the summer holidays? My uncle said he'd start teaching me on his farm when I'm there for a holiday.'

'I'll leave it up to your physios to decide when you're good to do something like that but I'm happy to sign you off to start physiotherapy sessions in the department here. They've got a hot swimming pool you're going to love and you'll get some one-on-one sessions in the gym as well.'

'Cool,' Michael said. 'I like swimming. Can I stop wearing my brace now, too?'

'Not just yet. I'll have a meeting with your physios before your next outpatient appointment and we'll talk about that then, okay?' He turned to Michael's mother. 'Have you got any questions or worries about how everything's going?'

She shook her head. 'That nurse practitioner in the ward has been so great. You know Molly?'

Hugh gave a single nod of agreement. He dropped his gaze to Michael's notes again so that he could hide the way it made him feel when he heard Molly's name.

Uncomfortable, that was what it was.

As if he'd done something wrong. Or stupid. Something that he should apologise for?

Something that he had the disturbing feeling that he might regret for the rest of his life?

He had pushed her away. They were simply colleagues now. He'd made sure they didn't meet by chance out of work hours. He'd even gone as far as not going surfing. Anywhere…

Because thinking about going surfing made him think about Taylors Mistake beach and that made him think about Molly.

'She called us every day when we were first at home.' The list of things that Molly had helped with felt like a muted background to Hugh's thoughts but he nodded occasionally, to make it look like he was listening. 'And if Mike ends up being a helicopter pilot it'll be Molly's fault.'

Oh…now he could see her in the ward on the day that Michael had been admitted. Taking the time to ease his fears and to make him feel special by telling him she'd saved the best bed for him where he'd be entertained by watching the helicopters come and go.

It was only a tiny example of how kind a person Molly Holmes was.

She'd made Hugh feel special too. As if he'd met the only person in the world who could understand what he'd gone through when he'd lost both his sister and his dog.

She had really cared about him and he'd pushed her away.

Yeah…he needed to apologise…

Hugh pasted a smile on his face. 'Is that what you want to do, Michael?'

'It was pretty cool, watching them taking off and landing on the roof,' he admitted. 'And I love flying…'

'I'll tell Molly she's inspired you,' Hugh said. 'I'm sure she'll think that's a brilliant plan.'

They weren't just empty words, he decided, as he gave Michael and his mother directions to get to the physiotherapy department and make their first appointments.

He would tell Molly at the first opportunity he got. It might even provide an opportunity for that apology that he needed to make.

Molly was later than she'd intended to be leaving the physiotherapy department after sharing Sophie's first walk with her prosthesis because she'd bumped into Michael and his mum and they'd had a chat.

She was in a bit of a rush, now, to get Oreo back to the van in the hospital car park and head home. Molly needed to pick Milo up from her mother's, take some time to admire Bella's puppies and play with them, of course, and she was hoping to still have enough daylight for a walk on the beach. She had her head down, sending a text to her mother to let her know she was finally on her way, when Molly thought she heard her name being called.

She hadn't imagined it because Oreo had suddenly gone on high alert with her ears pricked and every muscle primed for action.

And there it was again, coming from behind her.

'Molly...'

Two things happened in a tiny space of time as Molly swung her head to see Hugh coming towards her, framed by the backdrop of the hospital's main entrance.

Oreo—very uncharacteristically—did a U turn and took off, bounding towards Hugh as if he was a long-lost friend she couldn't wait to reconnect with.

And a car came racing along the stretch of road that led to both the car park entrance and the emergency department of Christchurch Children's Hospital.

Hugh's voice was much louder this time. 'Oreo...*no*...!'

Like it did in the movies, sometimes, everything became slow-mo and, to her horror, Molly could see it happen in excruciating clarity. Oreo had her focus so completely on Hugh she was unaware of the vehicle speeding towards her. A split second either way and it probably wouldn't have happened.

But it did.

Oreo ran in front of the car. She got hit square on her side and knocked flat. Even worse, the car went over the top of her and for another split second she vanished. Then she rolled out from beneath the back of the car as the driver slammed on the brakes.

And she wasn't moving.

At all.

* * *

The car screeched to a halt and the driver was starting to climb out of the car as Molly ran towards Oreo.

'Oh…my God…' The man was halfway out of the driver's seat, clearly distressed. 'I didn't see her… I've got my son in the car and he's having a bad asthma attack…'

Hugh arrived at the same time Molly did.

'*Go…*' he told the man. 'Get your son into the emergency department.'

The man drove off, his car door still swinging half open.

Molly sank to her knees. Oreo's eyes were only half open and she couldn't tell how well her beloved dog was breathing. She could see injuries that made her feel sick to her stomach. An open fracture to her front leg with bone visible. Missing skin and bleeding on her flank. A lot of bleeding. Molly's vision was blurring with tears and her breath felt stuck in her chest beneath an enormous weight.

Hugh had one hand on the wound. He put his other hand on Oreo's chest. 'She's breathing,' he told Molly. 'Her heart rate's strong but rapid— maybe two hundred beats per minute. We need to get her to a vet. *Stat…*'

We…?

Molly blinked to clear the tears in her eyes.

She could feel them rolling down her face as she looked up to meet Hugh's gaze. She wasn't alone in what felt like the worst moment of her life.

For just a heartbeat—a nanosecond—Molly remembered being on the beach that evening when everything had changed. When she'd known Hugh was confronted with memories of the worst moments of *his* life, when he'd lost everything that mattered the most to him. She remembered the silent message she'd tried so hard to send him.

You don't have to do this alone. I'm here... and... I love you...

It felt as if she was the one receiving that same message right now and it was cutting through her fear and shock.

'I need to keep pressure on this wound and stop any more blood loss,' Hugh said. 'Do you know if there's a vet clinic near here?'

'Yes…there's a big one only a few minutes' drive away.'

'Can you go and get your van?'

Hugh still hadn't broken that eye contact and it was giving Molly a strength she wouldn't have believed she had.

'*Yes…*'

'Hurry…'

Molly ran. She was out of breath and her hands were shaking so it took two attempts to get the key into the lock and open the driver's door. It took less than another minute to drive down the hospital's entranceway to where a small crowd had now gathered around Hugh and Oreo. Someone had supplied a dressing and bandages—maybe from ED—and it looked as if the bleeding was under control. Oreo was panting but her eyes were closed as if her level of consciousness was dropping and Molly had a moment of absolute clarity as she opened the back door of the van and Hugh gently picked Oreo up to put her on the soft blanket on the floor.

There was no way she could let Hugh come with her to the vet clinic.

No way she could put him through possibly having to witness Oreo being euthanised because her injuries were too severe to survive with any quality of life.

She loved him too much to put him through something he'd spent most of his life trying to escape.

'We'll be okay now,' she told Hugh. 'You don't need to come with us.'

'Are you sure?'

She loved that he looked so torn. That he was prepared to go through this for her sake. But she could see the flash of relief in his eyes when she gave a single but decisive nod of her head.

'I'm sure.'

* * *

Hugh stood where he was, watching the little green van speed off.

The crowd was beginning to disperse. A couple of people helpfully picked up the wrappers from the bandages and dressings he'd used to keep the worst of Oreo's wounds covered and under pressure to help stop the blood loss. He could hear the shocked tone of the things they were saying to each other but it sounded as if it were muted. That someone else was listening to it or it was a part of a dream. A nightmare.

'I know his kid was sick but he shouldn't have been going so fast.'

'His kid was sick. He wouldn't have been thinking about anything else.'

'And why was that dog here, anyway?'

'It had a coat on. Maybe it was a guide dog.'

'Its owner wasn't blind. She was driving a van!'

'I hope that kid's okay...'

'I hope the dog's okay...'

Hugh could have added to that conversation to echo those comments and say that *he* hoped Molly was okay.

But he didn't want to share his feelings with strangers.

He didn't want to think about them, either.

Maybe if he made himself move he could some-how wake up from this daytime nightmare.

For some reason Hugh turned to walk back into the hospital rather than continuing towards the car park. Because he couldn't imagine going home to stare at the walls of his apartment and think about what had just happened? Or maybe it was because he needed the comfort zone of being at work rather than in a personal space?

He got as far as the stairs he could take to get up to the level of his ward and his office but he didn't push the firestop door open. He pressed the button to summon a lift, instead, but he wasn't thinking about what he was doing or why he was doing it. His head was full of something else.

The knowledge that Molly couldn't possibly be anything like okay.

She *loved* Oreo. Adored her, even. She was able to love fiercely and without reservation and she could give everything she had—heart and soul—to the things she loved that much.

He'd been like that, once.

He'd loved Michelle like that.

And his mother.

And Fudge.

Before he knew just how destructive it could be to have your heart shattered in an instant. Or chipped away at slowly so that it felt like it was bleeding to death, the way it had when his mother had become lost for ever in the depths of her grief and depression.

But Molly knew how hard it was to lose someone or something you loved that much and yet she was still prepared to do it again. She had no hesitation in throwing herself into everything she chose to love in her life. To her family. To her dogs—her fur kids...

He could hear an echo of her voice.

It's unbearably hard to lose dogs...but, for me, it would be even harder to live without them...

She was that passionate about her job, as well. To those children she gave so much to in and out of her normal working hours, like she had when little Sam Finch was dying.

Maybe she would love *him* that much, if he ever let her get close enough. Or maybe she would have but he'd destroyed that possibility by pushing her away so decisively.

The ding announced the arrival of the lift. The doors opened and people got out. And then the doors closed again but Hugh hadn't stepped inside.

He was thinking about Sam again.

About how he'd known Molly wouldn't be okay and how he'd had that urge to go and find her. Not to tell her that she should have heeded his warning about the dangers of getting so involved.

He'd gone because he'd needed to see her.

To make sure she wasn't alone because...

...because he needed to *be* there with her.

And he finally knew why. It was because he *loved* her. As much as he'd ever loved anything in his entire life.

Hugh turned away from the lift. He was scrolling his phone to find the address of the closest veterinary hospitals.

He was running by the time he reached the car park.

He knew exactly where he was going now.

Where he needed to be.

CHAPTER TWELVE

THERE WAS NOTHING more Molly could do.

Staff from the veterinary hospital had rushed into the car park as soon as Molly stumbled through the doors, begging for help. They had carried Oreo into one of the clinic's treatment rooms and they were doing everything they could to help the badly injured dog.

It could have been a trauma team in the emergency department of Christchurch Children's Hospital working on a child who'd been rushed in by ambulance after being hit by a car, Molly thought as she listened to them going through a primary survey. It felt like she was watching from a huge distance even though she could almost have reached out and touched Oreo.

'Is her airway open?'

'Yes.'

'Is she breathing?'

'Tachypnoeic. Breath sounds reduced on the left side. Potential pneumothorax. Feels like at least one rib's fractured.'

'What's her heart rate?'

'Two hundred. Gums are pale. She's in shock.'

'Let's get an IV line in, please, and fluids up. Forty mils per kilo over the next fifteen minutes or so.'

'What's her weight?'

'I'd guess around twenty kilos.'

Molly knew it was eighteen kilos but the vet's guess was close enough. She couldn't make her lips work in time because they, along with the rest of her body, felt completely numb. Things were happening too fast and this was simply too huge. These strangers were fighting for Oreo's *life*…

'I think we should intubate and ventilate. Her oxygen saturation's dropping.'

'Is that external bleeding under control?'

'As soon as we've got her airway secured, we need to set up for X-rays. I want an abdominal ultrasound, too, thanks. We can't exclude major internal bleeding from a rupture with that mechanism of injury…'

They knew what they were doing, this team, as they worked swiftly and effectively to get Oreo's airway and breathing secured and fluids up to maintain her circulation and blood pressure. They started antibiotics, took X-rays of the fracture in her front leg and cleaned and dressed the wound on her flank. The ultrasound showed some free fluid that could be internal bleeding but, as the head vet explained, they wouldn't know the extent of all the damage until they got her into Theatre.

Oreo was heavily sedated and dosed with pain killers so she probably wasn't even aware of where she was or what was happening but Molly had to press her lips to the silky hair on her head and whisper something only her dog could hear before they took her away to Theatre. She had signed a consent form that included a statement to the effect that if it was clear that the likelihood of Oreo surviving or that her quality of life would be unacceptably diminished, they would not wake her up again.

A nurse took her back out to the waiting room. She touched Molly's arm and her expression couldn't have been more sympathetic.

'Is there someone I can call for you?'

Molly shook her head. She could have called for her mum or her brother or a friend to come and stay with her while she waited for the call that would tell her whether Oreo was still alive but she couldn't do it.

Not simply because she was still feeling so frozen.

She knew she would need all the comfort and understanding that her family could give her soon but, right now, there was only one person who would be able to hold her hand on a level that was so much deeper than merely physical.

Only one person who could touch her soul in a way that would give her the strength to get through anything.

Even this…

But she had pushed him away. She'd put up the same kind of barrier he'd put in place himself not so long ago. Except that she'd done it for very different reasons, hadn't she? She'd wanted to protect him from pain because she loved him *that* much.

He'd put the barriers up to protect himself…

Was that why Molly felt so utterly alone?

So…*lost*…?

'You could wait here but it could be hours,' the nurse said. 'We've got your number. I'll call you as soon as we know anything. It might help to be somewhere else. Or to go for a walk or something?'

But Molly shook her head again. She didn't want to leave.

But she didn't want to stay, either.

She had absolutely no idea what she wanted, to be honest.

Until she heard the doors sliding open behind her and heard a voice that filled the air around her and she could breathe it in and feel it settle close to her heart.

'I'll look after her,' Hugh told the nurse.

And then he folded Molly into his arms and she pressed her head into the hollow beneath his shoulder. She could feel the steady beat of his heart beneath her cheek.

'I've got you, sweetheart,' he murmured against her ear. 'I'm not going to let you go…'

There was a river that meandered along the foothills on the south side of the city and it had wide enough borders to provide walking tracks, picnic tables, children's playgrounds and lots of benches for people to sit and enjoy the kind of serenity that moving water and the green space of trees and grass could bestow.

Hugh would have preferred to take Molly to a beach to watch and listen to the waves rolling in but he knew she would hate to be taken too far away from where Oreo was fighting for her life. Luckily, like Christchurch Children's Hospital— a mile or two downstream—this veterinary hospital was just across the road from the river so Hugh led Molly across a small, pedestrian bridge to where there was a bench on the riverbank— a two-minute walk at most from the front doors of the veterinary hospital and he'd told the nurse where they would be. That way they could come and find Molly to give her any news, rather than making a more impersonal phone call.

For the longest time, they simply sat side by side. In silence.

There were ducks on the river who were diving to catch their dinner and then popping up again to bob on the surface like bath toys. People walked past, some walking their dogs, but they were too far away to intrude.

It was Molly who broke the silence.

'Thank you…' she said softly. 'For coming.'

'I had to,' Hugh said.

'No…' Molly shook her head. 'You didn't *have* to.' But her sideways glance was anxious. 'I hope you don't think what happened was your fault. I should have had Oreo on her lead. She's never run off like that before.'

'It was because I called you.'

'No…' Molly shook her head again but this time there was a poignant smile playing around her lips. 'It was because she loves you. She's been missing you.'

Hugh swallowed hard. 'I've been missing her. And you.'

Molly was staring at the ducks on the river again. 'Same…'

Hugh reached for Molly's hand and she let her fingers lace through his and be held. Silence fell again and he knew they were both thinking about what was going on in the operating room of the veterinary hospital across the river. About how much Oreo would be missed if she didn't make it through this surgery. This waiting period was more than anxiety. It felt like a practice run for grief.

'You told me once that grief is love that has nowhere to go,' he said softly. 'I know how over-whelming your love for Oreo is right now. I can *feel* it.'

Molly's voice had cracks in it. 'But you're so good at *not* feeling things like that. At protecting yourself.'

'I used to be,' he agreed quietly. 'And, if it ever got hard, all I needed to do was remind myself that grief can kill you, like it killed my mother. It didn't matter that I was there and I loved her. She just took herself somewhere else and never came back. She died of a broken heart but she never told me how bad it was.'

'Maybe she was trying to protect you,' Molly suggested. 'By shutting you away from her pain?'

'I didn't want to be shut away,' Hugh said. 'I wanted to help.'

'I know. I'm sorry…'

Hugh had to pull in a slow breath. 'I'm sorry, too…' he said.

'For Oreo?'

'Of course. But for more than that, too. For the way I've been shutting *you* away.'

'I pushed you,' Molly admitted. 'I pushed my

way into things that you wanted to keep private. I said things I shouldn't about you being selfish when you were only doing what you needed to do to protect yourself.'

'When I was coming to find you, I found myself remembering the day that Shelly died,' Hugh said quietly. 'Mostly, the way that Fudge refused to get off her bed. The look in his eyes that told me he knew what was happening and, no matter how hard it was, he didn't want to be anywhere else.'

Molly nodded. And brushed away a tear that rolled down her cheek.

Hugh squeezed her hand that he was still holding.

'I remembered you saying how hard it was to lose a dog but that it was even harder to live without them. That dogs have the ability to supply limitless, unconditional love.'

She nodded again. 'They do...'

'I think you do, too.' Hugh had to swallow past the lump in his throat. 'I never wanted to become dependent on any kind of love again after losing everything I cared the most about. I didn't think that I could even get close to feeling like it could even exist for me again.'

He could feel an odd prickling sensation at the back of his eyes.

'Until I met you,' he added.

He could feel Molly's fingers tightening around his own. Looking up, he found her gaze fixed on his face.

'Until I realised that you could not only un-derstand the kind of grief I went through with Shelly—and Fudge—but that you were still brave enough to get in there and do it all again. And... and I think that maybe you're right. That it is harder to live without that kind of love in your life. Emptier, anyway...'

'I think of love as being a kind of coin,' Molly said. 'There's lots of different kinds—or val-ues, I guess, like real coins. There are the ones for friends and siblings and others for, say, your mum or a child. And dogs, of course. And really special ones if you're lucky enough to find your soul mate.'

She paused to take a breath but Hugh didn't say anything. He knew she hadn't finished yet.

'They have two sides, too, like real coins,' Molly added. 'There's love on one side but there's grief on the other side and if it gets dropped and spins you don't know what side it's going to land on. And yeah...there are some coins you don't have a choice to hold, like your family, but there are others where you get the choice of whether or not you pick them up and it's safer not to, because some of them are the wrong coins and some of them might lead to heartbreak again, but if you don't pick them up, you'll never know the joy it can bring if you've found the one you were always meant to find—or were lucky enough to be given.' She offered him a smile. 'Like your Fudge coin?'

'I remember.' Hugh nodded. 'The joy I felt when I came home from school and Fudge would be there, lying just inside the gate, his ball between his paws. Waiting…just for me. And how it felt when he sat on the back step with me late at night sometimes and I could put my arms around him and hide my face in his hair while I cried…'

Oh, *God*… He was crying now. For the first time since the day his sister had died, he knew he was crying.

Okay…maybe he had been crying that day in the surf when he'd made the decision that he had to stay away from Molly—and Oreo—because he couldn't risk loving them and he wasn't going to risk hurting them. But it had been easy to think it was sea water.

This time, there was no hiding the fact that his walls had completely crumbled.

'I get that feeling with you,' he whispered. 'Only it's even bigger. I love you, Molly. And, when I touch you, I think I can feel a kind of love that's so big it's…well, it's a bit terrifying, that's what it is.'

* * *

Molly let go of his hand but only so that she could reach up and brush away the tears on Hugh's cheeks.

'You can feel it because it's there,' she said, softly. 'I do love you, Hugh. *So* much. I fell in love with you ages ago. Right about the time I heard about your sister and I knew there was a reason why you had walls up to stop anyone getting close to you.'

'My walls don't seem to be working any longer.' Hugh was blinking his tears back. 'I've tried to stay away from you and it's not working.' A corner of his mouth lifted. 'Do you really love me, Molly?'

'More than I can say.'

She still had her hand on his cheek as she lifted her chin and Hugh bent his head and their kiss was as tender as it was possible for any kiss to be. And then Molly pulled back.

'When they took Oreo into Theatre, the nurse asked me if she could call someone to be with me while I waited and I said "no" because there was only one person I wanted to be with me and I didn't want to call you. I couldn't ask you to do something this hard…for *me*…'

'I will always be with you,' Hugh said. 'Today and tomorrow and for ever. No matter how hard it is, I will always be here and I will always love you.'

'Oh…' Molly was going to cry again. She tried to smile instead. 'That sounds like it could be a wedding vow.'

'Maybe I'd better write it down.' Hugh was smiling, too. 'Just in case we need it one of these days.'

They hadn't noticed the figure coming across the bridge until the nurse from the veterinary hospital was close enough to clear her throat and warn them of her approach.

Molly's heart stopped. She felt Hugh's hand close around hers and then she felt a painful thump of her heart starting again. But she still couldn't breathe. Even though the nurse was smiling.

'Oreo's okay,' she said. 'She's come through the surgery like a champion and she hasn't lost her leg. We're going to keep her well sedated and in intensive care for a while but do you want to come and see her for a minute or two?'

Molly was already on her feet.

So was Hugh.

And his hand was still holding hers as if he had no intention of letting it go.

Ever…

'We do,' was all he said.

It was all he needed to say. Because that one tiny word said it all.

We...

Molly was never going to be alone again. She had found her soul mate.

EPILOGUE

Three years later...

'WHY DOES YOUR dog walk funny?'

'A long time ago, she had to have a big operation on her leg.'

'Like I'm going to have?'

'Just like you're going to have, darling.'

'But she got better?'

'Yes, she did.'

'Does it still hurt her? Is that why she holds her paw up like that?'

'Do you want to know a secret?'

The small boy lying on the bed nodded. He was reaching out to touch Oreo's nose and wasn't taking any notice of the anaesthetist who was getting ready to inject the sedative needed for this procedure.

'I think when Oreo was getting better from her operation she learned that if people thought she had a sore paw, she would get lots of cuddles.'

The child's eyes were drifting shut. 'I like cuddles…' he murmured.

His mother leaned closer to squeeze her son, but she was smiling at Molly. 'Thank you,' she whispered.

'You're so welcome.'

'It can't be easy making the time to do this when you've got a little one of your own to look after.'

Molly adjusted the warm, sleeping bundle that was her newborn daughter, tied close to her body in its comfortable sling. 'Oh, it's easy at this stage. It's when they get mobile that it gets harder. That's why I've got our toddler in the great crèche we have here. I'm so happy that I get to use that even when I'm on maternity leave.'

An ultrasound technician had manoeuvred her equipment into place and a nurse was ready with all the instruments and other materials that would be needed, including the jars to hold the fragments of bone tissue about to be collected. Molly moved Oreo away from the table as the surgeon who was about to do the bone biopsy moved towards the table. She knew he was smiling at his patient's mother by the way his eyes crinkled over the top of his mask.

'How are you feeling, Sue?'

'Okay. You were right—it's been so much easier having Molly and Oreo in here with us. I had no idea that dogs would be allowed somewhere like this.'

'Not only allowed. We encourage it.' Hugh was smiling at Molly as she prepared to slip out of the room. A heartbeat of time that was too relaxed and warm to be entirely professional. A beat of eye contact that was even more personal. 'We all love Molly and Oreo.'

Molly paused for a moment as the room's lights were dimmed enough to make the ultrasound images on the screen clearer and Hugh shifted his focus entirely onto the procedure he was about to perform.

She just wanted to let her gaze rest on her husband for a moment longer. To feel the sheer joy that this man was sharing every bit of this amazing life they were building together. That, so often, there was something extra special to be celebrated in the private moments they had together when their two adorable daughters were finally both asleep at the same time and Oreo and Milo just as content.

Like they had last week when Hugh had told her about his outpatient appointment with Michael, who'd come to ask him to contribute to the medical assessment he needed to gain the Class Two certificate that was a necessary part of the process of qualifying for his private pilot's licence. His parents had given him the first hours of his dual instruction in flying as his seventeenth birthday gift and, apparently, they were planning to invite Molly to his graduation ceremony.

And this afternoon, when Molly had gone to visit her ward before Oreo was scheduled to be the dogtor for this bone biopsy, she'd been lucky enough to catch a visit from Sophie Jacobs, who had been on her way to an appointment in the prosthetic department. The now cancer-free ten-year-old, who still had a smile that looked like it was Christmas, had wanted to show off the diploma she'd just received for passing her Grade Two ballet examination.

Molly couldn't wait to share that news with Hugh this evening.

No…actually, it wouldn't matter if she didn't have something interesting or exciting to share with him.

She would be just as happy to simply *be* with him.

Today, tomorrow and…for ever.

* * * * *